SO-BAH-356

ACCLAIM FOR
JIM THOMPSON

"The best suspense writer going, bar none." — *New York Times*

"My favorite crime novelist—often imitated but never duplicated." — Stephen King

"My man in crime fiction." — Jo Nesbø

"If Raymond Chandler, Dashiell Hammett, and Cornell Woolrich would have joined together in some ungodly union and produced a literary offspring, Jim Thompson would be it.... His work casts a dazzling light on the human condition." — *Washington Post*

"The master of the American groin-kick novel." — *Vanity Fair*

"Like Clint Eastwood's pictures it's the stuff for rednecks, truckers, failures, psychopaths, and professors.... One of the finest American writers and the most frightening, Thompson is on best terms with the devil. Read Jim Thompson and take a tour of hell." — *New Republic*

"The most hard-boiled of all the American writers of crime fiction." — *Chicago Tribune*

BOOKS BY JIM THOMPSON

The Alcoholics
A Swell-Looking Babe
After Dark, My Sweet
Bad Boy
The Criminal
Cropper's Cabin
The Getaway
The Golden Gizmo
The Grifters
Heed the Thunder
A Hell of a Woman
The Killer Inside Me
The Kill-Off
The Nothing Man
Nothing More than Murder
Now and on Earth
Pop. 1280
Recoil
The Rip-Off
Roughneck
Savage Night
South of Heaven
Texas by the Tail
The Transgressors
Wild Town

THE NOTHING MAN

JIM THOMPSON

MULHOLLAND BOOKS

LITTLE, BROWN AND COMPANY

NEW YORK   BOSTON   LONDON

The characters and events in this book are fictitious. Any similarity to real persons, living or dead, is coincidental and not intended by the author.

Copyright © 1954 by Jim Thompson, copyright © renewed 1982 by Alberta H. Thompson

Excerpt from *The Killer Inside Me* copyright © 1952 by Jim Thompson, copyright © renewed 1980 by Alberta H. Thompson

All rights reserved. In accordance with the U.S. Copyright Act of 1976, the scanning, uploading, and electronic sharing of any part of this book without the permission of the publisher constitute unlawful piracy and theft of the author's intellectual property. If you would like to use material from the book (other than for review purposes), prior written permission must be obtained by contacting the publisher at permissions@hbgusa.com. Thank you for your support of the author's rights.

Mulholland Books / Little, Brown and Company
Hachette Book Group
237 Park Avenue, New York, NY 10017
mulhollandbooks.com

Originally published in paperback by Dell Books, December 1954
First Mulholland Books paperback edition, August 2014

Mulholland Books is an imprint of Little, Brown and Company, a division of Hachette Book Group, Inc. The Mulholland Books name and logo are trademarks of Hachette Book Group, Inc.

The publisher is not responsible for websites (or their content) that are not owned by the publisher.

ISBN 978-0-316-40401-3
LCCN 2014938195

10 9 8 7 6 5 4 3 2 1

RRD-C

Printed in the United States of America

THE NOTHING MAN

I

Well, they are all gone now, all but me: all those clear-eyed, clear-thinking people—people with their heads in the clouds and their feet firmly on the ground—who comprise the editorial staff of the Pacific City *Courier*. Warmed with the knowledge of a day's work well done, they have retired to their homes. They have fled to the sweet refuge of their families, to the welcoming arms of brave little women and the joyous embrace of laughing kiddies. And with them has gone the clearest-eyed, clearest-thinking of them all, Dave Randall, none other than the *Courier*'s city editor.

He stopped by my desk on his way out, his feet firmly on the ground—or, I should say, the city room floor—but I did not look up immediately. I was too shaken with emotion. As you have doubtless suspected, I have a poet's heart; I think in allegories. And in my mind was an image of countless father birds, flapping their weary wings to the nests where the patient mother birds and the wee little birdies awaited them. And—and I say this unashamed—I could not look up. All the papa birds flapping toward their nests, while I—

Ah, well. I forced a cheery smile. I had my family; I was a member of the happy *Courier* family—clear-eyed, clear-thinking.

And what bride could be finer than my own, what better than to be wed to one's work?

Dave cleared his throat, waiting for me to speak; then he reached over my shoulder and picked up an overnight galley on my column, *Around the Town With Clinton Brown*. The *Courier* is generous in such matters, I should say. The *Courier* believes in giving its employees an opportunity to "grow." Thus, desk men may do reporting; reporters may work the desk; and rewrite men such as myself may give the fullest play to the talents which, on so many newspapers, are restricted and stunted by the harsh mandates of the Newspaper Guild.

We take no dictation from labor bosses. Our protector, our unfailing friend and counselor, is Austin Lovelace, publisher of the *Courier*. The door to his office is always open, figuratively speaking. One may always take one's problems to Mr. Lovelace with the assurance that they will be promptly settled. And without "outside interference."

But I shall touch on these things later. I shall have to touch upon them since they all figure, to an extent, in what the head-writers term the Sneering Slayer murders, and this is the story of those murders. For the nonce, however, let us get back to Dave Randall.

He laid the column galley back on my desk, clearing his throat again. He has always — well, almost always — had trouble in talking to me; and yet he insists on talking. One almost feels at times that he has a guilty conscience.

"Uh, working pretty late, aren't you, Brownie?"

"Late, Colonel?" I said. I had gained control of myself at last, and I gave him a brave, clear-eyed smile. "Well, yes and no. Yes, for a papa bird with a nest. No, for a restless, non-papa bird. My work is my bride and I am consummating our wedding."

"Uh...I notice your picture is pretty badly smudged. I'll order a new cut for the column."

"I'd rather you didn't, Colonel," I said. "I think of the lady birds, drawn irresistibly by my chiseled, unsmudged profile, their tail feathers spread in delicious anticipation. I think of their disappointment in the end—you should excuse the pun, Colonel. As a matter of fact, I believe we should dispense with my picture entirely, replace it with something more appropriate, a coat of arms say—"

"Brownie—" He was wincing. I had barely raised the harpoon, yet already he was wincing. And there was no longer any satisfaction in it for me—if there had ever been any—but I went on.

"Something symbolic," I said. "A jackass, say, rampant against two thirds of a pawnbroker's sign, a smug, all-wise-looking jackass. As for the device, the slogan—how is your Latin, Colonel? Can you give me a translation of the phrase, 'I regret that I had only his penis to give to my country'?"

He bit his lip, his thin face sick and worried. I took the bottle from my desk and drank long and thirstily.

"Brownie, for God's sake! Won't you ever give it up?"

"Yes," I nodded. "Word of honor, Colonel. Once this bottle is finished I shall not drink another drop."

"I'm not talking about that. Not just that. It's—everything else! You're getting too raw. Mr. Lovelace is bound to—"

"Mr. Lovelace and I," I said, "are spiritual brothers. We are as close as two wee ones in the nest. Mr. Lovelace would think my motives lofty, even should I turn into a pigeon and void on his snowy locks."

"You'll probably do it," said Dave, bitterly.

I hate to see a man bitter. How can you have that calm objectivity so necessary to literary pursuits if you are bitter?

"Yes, you'll do it," he repeated. "You won't stop until you're fired. You'll keep on until you're thrown out, and I have to—"

"Yes?" I said. "You mean you'd feel it necessary to leave also? How touching, Colonel. My cup runneth over with love—of, need I say, a strictly platonic nature."

I offered him a drink, jerking the bottle back as he tried to knock it from my hands. I took a drink myself and advised him to flee to the bosom of his family. "That is what you need, Colonel," I said. "The cool hand of the little woman, soothing away the day's cares. The light of love and trust that shines from a kiddie's—"

"Goddam you, shut up!"

He yelled it at the top of his lungs. Then he was bending over my desk, bracing himself with his hands, and his eyes and his voice were tortured with pleading and helplessness and fury. And the words were pouring from his mouth in a half-coherent babble.

Goddammit, hadn't he said it was a mistake? Hadn't he admitted it was a boner a thousand times? Did I think he'd deliberately send a man into a field of anti-personnel mines?... It was a tragedy. It was a hell of a thing to happen to any man, and it must be ten times as hard when the guy was young and good-looking, and—and it was his fault. But what more could he do than he'd already done? What did I want him to do?

He choked up suddenly. Then he straightened and headed for the door. I called after him. "A moment, Colonel. You didn't let me finish."

"You're finished!" He whirled, glaring at me. "That's one thing you're finished with. I warn you, Brownie, if you ever again call me Colonel, I'll—I'll—Well, take my tip and don't do it!"

"I won't," I said. "That's what I wanted to tell you. I'm cutting it all out. Everything. After all, it was just one mistake in a war full of mistakes. You'll never have any more trouble with me, Dave."

He snorted and reached for the door. He paused and looked at me, frowning uncertainly. "You—you almost sound like you meant that."

"I do. Every word of it, Dave."

"Well"—he studied me carefully—"I don't suppose you do, but—"

He grinned tentatively, still studying me. Slowly the suspicion went out of his eyes and the grin stretched into a broad, face-lighting smile. "That's great, Brownie! I'm sorry I blew my top a moment ago, because I do know how you feel, but—"

"Sure," I said. "Sure you do. It's all right, Dave."

"Why don't you knock off for the night? Come out to the house with me? I'll open a bottle, have Kay cook us up some steaks. She's been after me to bring you home to dinner."

"Thanks," I said. "I guess not tonight. Got a story I want to finish."

"Something of your own?"

"We-ell, yes," I said. "Yes, it's something of my own. A kind of melodrama I'm building around the Sneering Slayer murders. I suppose it'll baffle hell out of the average who-dunit reader, but perhaps he needs to be baffled. Perhaps his thirst for entertainment will impel him to the dread chore of thinking."

"Great!" Dave nodded earnestly. He hadn't, of course, heard anything I'd said. "Great stuff!"

He was looking happier than I'd seen him for a long time. I think he'd have looked happy even if I'd taken him up on the dinner invitation.

"Well—ha, ha—don't work all night," he said.

"Ha, ha," I said. "I'll try not to."

He clapped me on the back, clumsily. He said good night and I said good night, and he left.

I studied the page in my typewriter, ripped it out and put in another one.

I had got off on the wrong foot. I had begun the story with Deborah Chasen when, naturally, it had to begin with me. Me—sitting alone in the city room, with a dead cigarette butt in my lips and an almost full quart of whisky on my desk.

The two Teletype machines began to click and clatter—first the A.P.'s, then the U.P.'s. I strolled over and took a look at them.

Pacific City, in the words of our publisher, is a "city of homes, churches, and people"—which translated from its chamber-of-commerce *lingua franca* means that it is a small city, a nonindustrial city, and a city where little goes on, ordinarily, of much interest to the outside world. The *Courier* is the only newspaper. The wire services do not maintain correspondents here but are covered, when coverage is necessary, by our staffers.

I ripped the yellow flimsies from the Teletypes and read:

LOS ANG 6OIPM SPL AP TO COURIER
PACITY CHF DET LEM STUKEY REPTD MISSING
OVER TWENTYFOUR HOURS. TRUE? UNUSUAL?

POSSIBLE CONNECTION SNEERING SLAYER CASE?
LET'S HEAR FROM YOU COURIER. THATCHER AP LA

         LA CAL 603 PM UP TO COUR
RADIO REPTS DETEC CHF LEM STUKEY MISSING.
HOW ABOUT THIS COURIER? WHY NOT
MENTIONED ANY YOUR EDITIONS? UNIMPORTANT?
OFTEN MISSING? ANSWER DALE (SIG) LOS ANG UP.

I tossed the flimsies into a wastebasket and strolled over to a window.... True? Yes, the report was true enough. Pacific City's Chief of Detectives Lem Stukey *had* been missing for more than a day.... Unusual? We-ell, hardly. The police department wasn't alarmed about it. They hadn't been able to locate him in any of the blind pigs or whorehouses where he usually holed up, but he could have found a new place. Or, perhaps, someone had found a place for him....

Anyway, the wire services couldn't expect us to follow up on a query at this hour. We were an afternoon paper. Our "noon" edition hit the streets at ten in the morning, our "home" at noon, and our "late final" — a re-plate job — at three in the afternoon. That was more than three hours ago, so to hell with A.P. and U.P. To hell with them, anyway.

I stared out the window — out and down to the street, ten stories below. And I was sad, more than sad, even bitter. And all over nothing, nothing at all, really. Merely the fact that the last line of this story will have to be written by someone else.

I turned from the window and marched back to my desk. I successfully matched myself for two drinks and received another on the house.

I looked back through what I had written. Then, I lowered my hands to the keys and began to type:

The day I met Deborah Chasen was the same day I got the letter from the Veterans' Administration. It was around nine of a morning a couple of months ago, and Dave Randall...

2

Dave had, on that morning, brought it over to my desk. He stood lingering a moment afterward, trying to look friendly and interested. He mumbled something about "Good news, I hope," and I opened the letter.

It was, as I've said, from the Veterans' Administration. It announced that my disability compensation was being increased to approximately eighty dollars a month.

I shoved back my chair. I stood up, clicked my heels together, and gave Dave a snappy salute.

"Official communication, sir! Sergeant Brown respectfully requests the colonel's instructions!"

"Carry on." He looked nervously around the office, that sickly smile on his face. "Brownie, I wish —"

"Thank you, Colonel. The hour for the morning patrol approaches. Do I have the colonel's permission to —?"

"Do any goddamned thing you want to," he said, and he strode back to his desk.

I sat down again. I winked at Tom Judge, who worked the rewrite desk opposite me. I gave him a smile, a very cheery smile considering that I hadn't had a drink since breakfast.

Tom didn't smile back. "Why do you keep riding him?" He scowled. "Why make things tough on a good guy?"

"Why, Tom," I said. "You mean you and the colonel are— like *that?*"

"I mean I like him. I mean if I were in his place I'd straighten you out or kick your ass out of here. Boy"—he shook his head disgustedly—"talk about justice! Where the hell do you get off drawing a pension anyway?"

"It is puzzling," I said, "isn't it? Obviously I am not disabled for employment. Obviously I have suffered no disfigurement. I am even more handsome than on the day I was born, and my mother boasted—with considerable veracity, I believe—that I was the prettiest baby in town."

His eyes narrowed. "I get it. You're a fairy, huh?"

"Is that an assertion," I said, "or merely a surmise?"

"Don't think I'm afraid of you, Brown!"

"Aren't you?" I said. "Then perhaps you'd like to do something about my statement, made herewith, that you are a nosy, dull-witted son-of-a-bitch and a goddamned lousy news-paperman."

His face went white and he made motions at getting up from his chair. I got up and walked into the john.

A moment later he followed me in.

I could see that he was still sore, but he was trying to cover up. He would wait for a better time to pay me off.

"Look, Brown. I didn't mean t-to—"

"And I," I said, "apologize for calling you a son-of-a-bitch."

"About the pension, Brownie. Not that it's any of my business but—well, I guess it must have something to do with your nerves, huh?"

"That's it," I nodded soberly. "That's it exactly, Tom. A considerable portion of the nerves — kind of a nerve center — was completely destroyed."

I watched him carefully, afraid for a moment that I might have said too much, wondering what he would do — and what I would do — if the truth did dawn on him. Because there is something hideously funny about a thing of that kind. People laugh about it, privately perhaps, but they laugh. They give you sympathetic smiles and glances, their faces tight with laughter restrained. And even when they do not laugh you can hear them ... *Poor guy! What a hell of a — ha, ha, ha — I wonder what he does when he has to ...?*

You can't work. You can't live. You can't die. You are afraid to die, afraid of the complete defenselessness to laughter that death will bring.

But I needn't have worried about Tom Judge. He lacked the inquiring mind, the ability to follow up on a lead. He was, to mention a statement I had not retracted, a goddamned lousy newspaperman.

"Gosh, I'm sorry, Brownie. I guess that would make you pretty edgy. I still think you're pretty tough on Dave, but —"

I told him I didn't mean anything by it. "Not only is he my friend," I said, "but I respect him professionally. I wouldn't want to embarrass him by repeating the compliment, but Dave strikes me as typifying the genus *Courier*. Clear-eyed, clear-thinking, his feet firmly on the ground and his head —"

Tom laughed halfheartedly. "Okay," he said, "you win."

He returned to the rewrite bank.

I, because the *Courier*'s first deadline was past, went out on my morning patrol.

13

It was one of my better patrols. The officer of the day was at his post, and the heavy artillery stood waiting and ready.

"All secured?" I said.

"All secured," said Jake, the Press Club bartender.

"Proceed with maneuvers," I said.

He bent his wrist smartly. Bottle tilted over glass in a beautifully executed movement.

"Excellent," I said. "Now, I think we shall have close-order drill."

"Beggin' your pardon, sir, but—"

"Yes?"

"You only had—I mean you ain't completed the barrage."

"A new tactic," I said. "The remainder of the barrage will follow the drill."

"Okay. But if you fall on your face, don't—"

"Forward, *march!*" I said.

He lined three one-ounce shot glasses up on the bar, placed a two-ounce glass at the end of the line, and filled all four.

I disposed of them with dispatch and dipped into the bowl of cloves. "Reports or inquiries?" I said.

"I don't know how you do it," he said. "I swear, Mr. Brown, if I tried that I'd—"

"Ah," I said, "but I have youth on my side. Wondrous youth, with the whole great canvas of life stretching out before me."

"You always drink like that?"

"What's it to you?" I said, and I went back to the office.

I was experiencing that peculiar two-way pull that had manifested itself with increasing frequency and intensity in recent months. It was a mixture of calm and disquiet, of resignation and frantically furious rejection. Simultaneously I wanted to lash out at everything and do nothing about anything. The logical result of the conflict should have been stalemate, yet somehow it was not working out that way. The positive emotions, the impulse to act, were outgrowing the others. The negative ones, the calm and resignation, were exercising their restraining force not directly but at a tangent. They were not so much restrictive as cautionary.

They were pulling me off to one side, moving me down a course that was completely out of the world, yet of it.

I wondered if I was drinking too much.

I wondered how it would be — how I would manage to eat and sleep and talk and work: how to live — if I drank less.

I decided that I wasn't drinking enough, and that henceforth I should be more careful in that regard.

Dave Randall looked at me nervously as I sat down. Tom Judge jerked his head over his shoulder in a way that meant that Mr. Lovelace had arrived.

"And, Brownie," he leaned forward, whispering, "you should've seen the babe he had with him!"

"How, now," I said. "Much as it pains me, I shall have to report the matter to Mrs. Lovelace. The marriage vows are not to be trifled with."

"Boy, for some of that you could report me to my wife!"

"Let me catch you," I said, sternly, "and I shall."

It was an average morning, newswise. I did a story on the Annual Flower Show and another on the County Dairymen's convention. I rewrote a couple of wire stories with a local twist and picked up a few items for my column. So it went. That was the sort of thing—and about the only sort of thing—that got into the *Courier*.

Mr. Lovelace frowned on what he termed the "negative type" of story. He was fond of asserting that Pacific City was the "cleanest community in America," and he was very apt to suspect the credibility of reporters who produced evidence to the contrary. I could have done it and got away with it. For reasons that will become obvious, I held a preferred place in the "happy *Courier* family." But I was temporarily content with the *status quo,* and there was no one else. It had been years since any topflight reporter had applied for a job on the Pacific City *Courier*.

With my last story out of the way, I began to feel those twinges of mental nausea that always herald the arrival of my muse. I felt the urge to add to my unfinished manuscript, *Puke and Other Poems*.

I rolled paper into my typewriter. After some preliminary fumblings around, I began to write:

> *Lives of great men, lives en masse*
> *Seem a stench and cosmic ruse.*
> *Take my share, I'll take a glass*
> *(no demi-tasse—it has to knock me on my ass)*
> *Of booze.*

Not good. Definitely not up to Omar, or, perhaps I should say, Fitzgerald. I tried another verse:

> *Sentience, my sober roomer,*
> *Steals my warming cloak of bunk*

(I'm sunk, sunk, sunk.)
Leaves me an impotent assumer
Of things that I can take when drunk.

Very bad. Far worse than the first stanza. *Assumer*—what kind of word was that? And when was I ever actually drunk? And the wretched, sniveling self-pity in that *sunk, sunk, sunk*. . . .

I ripped the paper out of the typewriter and threw it into the wastebasket.

I didn't do it a bit too soon, either.

Mr. Lovelace wasn't a dozen feet away. He was heading straight toward me, and the "babe" Tom Judge had mentioned was with him.

I don't know. I never will know whether she was a little slow on the uptake, a little dumb, as, at first blush, I suspected her of being, or whether she was merely tactless, unusually straightforward, careless of what she said and did. I just don't know.

I gave Mr. Lovelace a big smile, including her in the corner of it. I complimented him on his previous day's editorial and asked him if he hadn't been losing weight and admired the new necktie he was wearing.

"I wish I had your taste, sir," I said. "I guess it's something you have to be born with."

No, I'm not overdrawing it. It doubtless seems that I am, but I'm not. He couldn't be kidded. However good you said he was, it wasn't ever quite so good as he *thought* he was.

I poured it on, and he stood beaming and rocking on the balls of his feet, nodding at the woman as if to say, "Now, here's a man who knows the score." Even when she burst out laughing, he didn't catch on.

He looked at her a little startled. Then the beam came back to his face and he chuckled. "Uh—just finished telling Mrs. Chasen a little story. Kind of a delayed punch, eh, Mrs. Chasen?"

She nodded, holding a handkerchief over her mouth. "I'm s-sorry, but—"

"Nothing to be sorry about. Often affect people that way.... Uh, by the way, Mrs. Chasen, this is the Mr. Brown I spoke to you about. Come along with us, eh, Brown?"

I followed them out into the reception room. "Mrs. Chasen," he explained, "is a very dear friend of ours—uh—of Mrs. Lovelace and myself. Unfortunately—uh—we did not expect Mrs. Chasen's visit and Mrs. Lovelace is out of town, and—uh—well, you know my situation, Brown."

"Tied up every second of the day," I said promptly. "Not a moment to call your own. Perhaps it's not my place to say it, Mrs. Chasen, but there isn't a busier man in Pacific City than Mr. Lovelace. The whole town leans on him. Because he is strong and wise, they—"

She started laughing again, staring at him with narrowed, unblinking eyes. And it was a nice laugh to hear, despite the undertone of contempt. And the way it made her tremble— *what* it trembled—was pleasant to watch.

Mr. Lovelace waited, smiling, of course, but with a nervous glance at the foyer clock. "So if you'll—uh—take over, Brown," he resumed. "You know. Show Mrs. Chasen our local points of interest, and—uh—play the host, eh?"

I knew what he meant. I knew exactly where Mrs. Chasen stood. She was an acquaintance of his and his wife's, a friend, perhaps, of a friend of theirs. And as such, she could not be given the fast brush-off. But she was certainly not their very dear friend. She wasn't because Mrs. Lovelace was *not* out of town, and he, Mr. Lovelace, was about as busy as the zipper on an old maid's drawers.

The Grade-C Tour. That was what Mrs. Chasen was supposed to get. A drive around the city, a highball or two, a meal in a not-too-expensive place, and a firm shove onto her train.

"I understand, sir," I said. "I'll show Mrs. Chasen what we mean when we call this the Friendly City! Just leave everything to me, Mr. Lovelace, and don't worry about a thing. You have far too many cares as it is."

"Uh — ha, ha — excellent, Brown. Oh, don't bother to come back today. Make a holiday of it. You can make the time up some other day."

"Do you see?" I turned to Mrs. Chasen, spreading my hands. "Is it any wonder we all love Mr. Lovelace?"

"Let's go," she said. "I need some fresh air."

If she'd been balancing a glass of water on her head, she wouldn't have spilled a drop with the nod she gave him. She turned abruptly and stepped onto the elevator.

I studied her, as best I could, on the way down to the street. And I liked what I saw, but I couldn't say why I liked it.

She wasn't any youngster — around thirty-five, I'd say. Added up feature by feature, she was anything but pretty. Corn-colored, almost-coarse hair, pulled back from her head in a horse's tail; green eyes that were just a shade off center; mouth a little too big. Assessed individually, the parts were all wrong, but when you put them all together you had a knock-out. There was something inside of her, some quality of, well, fullness, of liveness, that reached out and took hold of you.

When she stepped from the elevator, I saw that she toed in a little, her ankles were over-thin, the calves of her legs larger than the norm. But it was all right on her. On her it looked good. She preceded me to the street, the outsize hips swinging on the too-slender waist—or was it the slenderness of the waist that made her hips seem outsize?

One thing was certain, there was nothing at all wrong with Mrs. Chasen's bank balance. Not, that is, unless she'd given Saks Fifth Avenue and I. Magnin a hell of a kidding.

We reached the sidewalk and I started to take her by the elbow. She turned and looked up into my face.

"Have you," she said, "been drinking, Mr. Brown?"

"Why," I said, drawing away a little, "what makes you think I—why do you ask that?"

I didn't know what to say. The question had caught me completely off guard, and I still couldn't make up my mind whether she was stupid or only appeared to be.

As I say, I never could make it up.

"It's pretty early in the day to be drinking," I hedged.

"Not for me," she said, "under the circumstances. I'm going to have a drink, Mr. Brown. Several drinks, in fact. And you can come along or not come along, just as you please. As far as I'm concerned, you and your dear Mr. Lovelace—"

"Tut," I said. "Tish and pish, Mrs. Chasen. You have just said a naughty word, and there is only one thing to be done. We shall have to wash out your mouth."

"What" — she laughed a little nervously — "what do you —?"

"Come, Mrs. Chasen," I said. "Come with me to the Press Club."

I made a Charles Boyer face, and she laughed again. Not nervously, now. Rather, I thought, hungrily.

"Well, come *on!*" she said.

3

She leaned back in the booth, her green eyes crinkled and shiny with laughter, her breasts under the sheer white blouse shivering and shaking. I'd used to visualize breasts like those, but I never thought I'd live to see any. I'd considered them — well, you know — physically impractical. Something that looked very good in the blueprint stage, but impossible of achievement.

It just went to show — as Mr. Lovelace often remarked. Yes, sir, here was the proof; there was no problem too big for American genius and know-how.

". . . You crazy thing, Brownie! Do you always talk so crazy?"

"Only with people I love, Deborah. Only with you and Mr. Lovelace."

"You said it, Brownie! You said it that time!"

"So I did," I said, "and I shall take my punishment with my elbows firmly on the table. . . . Close-order drill?"

"With a barrage, Brownie! A *big* barrage!"

"Jake," I called, "advance with artillery."

Perhaps she hadn't been too tactful about it, but she'd had a right to be sore at Mr. Lovelace. Her late husband, late and elderly *("but he was a fine man, Brownie; I liked him a lot"),* had been an oil man. The Lovelaces had often visited them at their

22

place in Oklahoma. Then, six months ago, her husband had died, and she had found herself with a great deal of money and even more than she knew what to do with.... Money and time and a growing suspicion that she was not highly regarded in the circles she had formerly moved in. *("And why not, Brownie? I was good to him. I waited on him hand and foot for ten years.")*

She had fought back; she had delivered two snubs for every one she received. But you lose at that game, even when you win. There is no satisfaction in it. Finally, she had begun to travel—she was on her way to the Riviera now—and today she had stopped off here. And Lovelace, of course, had given her the firmest brush-off of all. *("But I'm glad I stopped, Brownie. You know?")* She was lonely as hell, though not the kind to admit it. The chances were that she would always be lonely. Because that manner of hers—whatever its motivation—was not something that would ordinarily win friends and influence people.

I had a hunch that she had even got under the Lovelace hide.

I stole a glance at my wrist watch and looked back at her. Thus far, she was holding her drinks very well. But train time was four hours away—she was catching the four-fifteen into Los Angeles. So it seemed to me that some food was indicated.

I picked up a menu, turned it right side up, and started to pass it across the table.

"I'll," she said, "have the hot turkey sandwich with mashed potatoes and buttered asparagus."

I nodded. "That sounds—Say, how did you know that was on the menu?"

"I read it." She smiled, pleased as a child with herself.

"Upside down? And sitting way over there?"

23

"Uh-huh. My eyes are wond—I mean, I have very good eyesight."

"In that case," I said, "you had better order the steak. You will be the only person in history ever able to see a Press Club steak."

We had the turkey sandwiches. I bought a bottle from Jake, and we got my car off the parking lot.

"Where are we going, Brownie?" she said. Then, before I could answer: "I know something about you."

"I was afraid of that," I said. "Yes, officer, you have the right person. I am actually Tinka Tin Nose, girl insect exterminator."

"You're sad."

"Why wouldn't I be with a name like that?"

"I know. You want to know how I know?"

"I've already told you."

"Crazy!" She gave it up. "Where did you say we were going?"

"Well, we have several points of interest. Ensconced in the basement of the public library is the largest collection of Indian artifacts in southeast Pacific County. Why, they have a *metate* there that actually makes your hands itch for a pot, and—"

"Pooh!"

"Check! You're a thousand per cent on the ball, D.C., and let me be the first to congratulate the new manager of our Pooh division.... How about a son-of-a-bitch? Would you like to see the world's biggest son-of-a-bitch, Deborah?"

"I thought I'd met him this morning."

"Sharp!" *Or was she?* "But this guy is in another class. He's our Chief of Detectives here, and—No sale?"

It wasn't. Obviously, and I say this in all modesty, she was quite content with the company present.

"Well," I said, "I'll have to take you some place. I may be asked to account for my time. What about a visit to our city animal shelter?"

"Animal shelter!" She wrinkled her nose. "Double pooh!"

"It's a nice long ride," I said carelessly. "Way out in the country, you know. I think you might enjoy it."

"Oh?" She sidled a glance at me, then nodded firmly. "I think I might, too."

That, then, was the way it happened. And, as you can see, there was nothing sinister about it, nothing premeditated. That trick she'd pulled in the Press Club — reading upside down and backward — had made no real impression on me. I hadn't been even mildly interested in why she thought I was sad.

We drove out to the shelter — well, call it dog pound, if you like — stopping at intervals for drills, bombardments, and barrages. By the time we reached our destination the bottle was empty, and Saks, Magnin, et al. knew little about the anatomy of Mrs. Chasen that I didn't know.

She was a little mussed. She was happy as all hell. I'd brought her back into the human race again, and her heart was right in her eyes. She could carry on by herself from now on. The ice was broken, and she'd be all right — as right, at any rate, as she could be. Much righter than she had been.

... The shelter was — and is — supported by donations; rather, I should say, it was supposed to be supported by them. Because the cash that came in wasn't half enough to operate the place decently. If Mr. and Mrs. Peablossom, the old couple who superintended the shelter, hadn't donated most of their wages, the dogs would have been completely starved instead of the two thirds starved that they usually were.

Mrs. Peablossom insisted on fixing tea for us, and afterward the old gentleman walked us out to the gate of the compound.

"I just don't know what we're going to do, Mr. Brown," he fretted. "The kennels have fallen to pieces. We have to let them run loose there in the court—and they keep coming in, more and more of them, and I can't bear to have them put to sleep—poor homeless fellows—but hardly anyone adopts a dog any more, and..."

He rambled on worriedly, while Deborah and I stood looking through the wire-mesh gate. There must have been two hundred dogs in there, closed in by the six-foot-high wall. They lay panting on the hot, shadeless pavement or milled around listlessly, pawing and sniffing hopelessly at the twigs that had blown over the wall.

I fumbled at my wallet, then shoved it back into my pocket. "I'm a little short of funds today, Mr. Peablossom, but—"

"That's quite all right, Mr. Brown. You've done far too much already."

"But *I* haven't done anything," said Deborah, and she opened her purse. She took out a fifty-dollar bill and handed it to him.

"Bless you!" The old man almost wept. "Thank you so much, Mrs. Chasen. Do you have dogs of your own?"

"No," she said. "I don't like dogs." She saw my frown. "I mean I'm afraid of them. A big dog knocked me down when I was a little girl and I never got over it. I've been terrified by them ever since."

I reached up to lift the hasp of the gate, but Mr. Peablossom caught my arm. "I don't believe you'd better go in today, Mr. Brown. The dogs are so hungry, and—"

"You think they're *that* hungry?"

"Well," he hesitated, looking apologetically at Deborah, "you know how it is with dogs, Mr. Brown. They can smell fear. It makes them worse than they might be ordinarily."

"I know," I said. "Well, we've got to be going, anyway. Mrs. Chasen has less than an hour to catch her train."

The old man saw us out to the car and stood waving until we were out of sight. Deborah leaned back in the seat, looking at me out of the corner of her eyes. "Brownie—"

"Yes?" I said.

"Do you—do you think I'm pretty?"

"No," I said. "You're too big, too little, too something every way I look at you, so you can't be pretty. What you are is just the damnedest, delightfulest chunk of woman I ever laid eyes on."

She sighed comfortably. "You really mean that, don't you?"

"Every word."

"And you like me? You know, Brownie? *Like?*"

"Like isn't quite the word," I said. "I'm crazy about you. Almost any man would be if you didn't scare him off. Which reminds me, Deborah..."

I suggested several ways by which she could do herself a favor: thinking before she spoke; aiming her laugh in some direction other than a person's face.

"Would you like me better that way, Brownie?"

"I like you just as you are," I said. "But I'm out of the picture. You're leaving and—"

"Leave with me, Brownie."

"Wha-at?" I jerked the car back onto the road in the nick of time. "Why, Mrs. Chasen, are you suggesting—?"

"Anything! Any way you want it, darling. I'd like to have you marry me, but—"

"But—but, honey!" I shook my head. "That's crazy! You don't know anything about me."

"Yes, I do. All I need to know."

I laughed shakily. The whisky was wearing off. My nerves were rising on edge, slicing up saw-toothed through the skin.... *All you need to know, eh? What do you know, anyway? That I can spiel the crap until your head spins? Why not? That I'm hot as a two-dollar pistol? Why not? I spiel it out to keep from drowning in it, and I was only emasculated—only!—not castrated....*

"You'll feel different tomorrow," I said. "Let's fact it, Deborah, we've had quite a bit to drink today."

"I want you to come with me, Brownie."

"No," I said. "Now drop it, will you? It's too damned idiotic to talk about."

"Then I'll stay here. I won't take my train."

"I said to drop it!" I snapped. "Of course you'll take your train. You've got a drawing-room bought and paid for. You've got your steamship passage. You're going to get on that train and—"

"Not without you," she said calmly. "Either you go, or I stay."

"I tell you, you can't! I can't! We hardly know each other. I haven't got anything but my job, and you—"

"Uh-huh," she nodded pleasantly. "I have plenty for both of us."

"B-But—dammit, people just don't do those things!"

"Pooh on people," she said.

It was like fighting something that wasn't there, something you couldn't believe in fighting—fighting yourself. She'd seemed as lost as I was, and it had been so long, so very long since I'd let myself touch a woman. I'd wanted to help her, shove her back into the mainstream of life that I could never be part of. And...

We were entering the edge of town. I slowed the car slightly. I made my voice harsh.

"All right, Mrs. Chasen. You won't let me do it the nice way, so we'll have to make it the other. I don't like you. I don't like your looks. You're stupid. You're cockeyed. I haven't seen hair like yours since I stopped riding horses. You've got a can on you like a whale, and I wouldn't get near that topside of yours in a high wind for all the—"

"B-Brownie! S-Stop!"

I stopped.

"I'm sorry," I said. "I don't enjoy talking to you this way. You were just a job with me—an assignment—and I tried to— Goddam you!" I said.

For she was laughing. Her head was thrown back and the green eyes were crinkled and flashing, and that topside I'd mentioned was trembling and shivering. She was laughing all over. I could almost see the naked, rippling flesh, feel it shivering against mine, while the green eyes looked up into mine. Hot, then curious. And at last pitying and disgusted.

My hands on the steering wheel were wet with sweat.

"You're so funny, Brownie!"

"Yeah," I said. "Very funny. I even keep myself in stitches."

She put her hand on my knee, gave it a quick, firm squeeze. "Funny and sad," she said. "But you won't be sad with me. I'll make you the happiest man in the world."

"There's just one way you can do that," I said. "Get on your goddamned train and get out of town, and don't come back."

"Huh-uh," she said. "Now, you park right here and we'll go in and get my bags."

We parked. I took her by the shoulders and turned her around facing me.

"No, Brownie"—she tried to squirm away—"there's not a bit of use in telling me that my—my—"

"I'm not," I said. "I'm telling you I'm nuts about you. I think perhaps I even love you. But—well, call me any name you like. Think what you want to. I thought we'd just have a high old time together, and then you'd go your way and I'd go mine. So—I didn't see how it would make any difference. But—"

I didn't have to say it. All the laughter went out of her eyes, and she turned slowly away from me. "That's—?" She changed the question into a statement. "That's true, Brownie."

"It's true. We're separated, but we're still married. She'd never give me a divorce."

"Well..." She fumbled for the door handle.

"I'm sorry, Deborah."

She shrugged, and the horsetail of corn-colored hair brushed against her shoulders. "D-Don't be," she said. "Don't be sad, Brownie. That's the way it is, so...th-that's the way it..."

She got out and walked toward the station, and she didn't look back.

4

I may be wrong—I have been wrong about so many things—but I can't recall ever hearing or knowing of a son-of-a-bitch who did not do all right for himself. I'm talking about *real* sons-of-bitches, understand. The Grade-A, double-distilled, steam-heated variety. You take a man like that, a son-of-a-bitch who doesn't fight it—who knows what he is and gives his all to it—and you've really got something. Rather, *he's* got something. He's got all the things that are held out to you as a reward for being a non-son-of-a-bitch. For being unlike Lem Stukey, Chief of Detectives of the Pacific City police department.

He poured himself another drink, shoved the bottle across his desk toward me, and gestured with his glass. He was a good-looking guy—gigolo-ish good-looking. With a little less beef on his belly and a lot less larceny in his heart, he might have been an instructor in a dollar-a-lesson dance academy.

"I don't make you, Brownie," he said. "I just don't dig you at all, keed. Ain't I always treated you right? You ever ask me for anything you didn't get? Hell, I try to be a pal to you, and—"

"Stuke," I said. "Will you shut up for a minute?"

"But—well, sure, Brownie. Go right ahead."

"It's this way, Stuke. I'm immune, know what I mean? I've

developed a tolerance for sons-of-bitches. I can drink with you and enjoy it. I can let you do me a little favor without having the slightest desire to puke. In a sort of hideous way, I actually like you. But—"

"I like you, too, Brownie. You're my kind of people."

"Now, let's not carry this too far," I said. "But speaking of favors, Stuke, I do you one every day. Every time I sit down at my typewriter without writing that Lem Stukey is the chief pimp, gambler, all-around and overall racketeer of Pacific City I'm doing you a favor. And any time you think I'm not—"

"Brownie!" He spread his hands. "Did I say no? I know you could blast me. You're the only guy that could. From what I hear, you could maybe write a story that old lovey drawers was beating his own wife, and he'd see that it went on the front page.... I *know*, see? I got the highest appreciation for you friendship. I know what you can do, or I wouldn't be asking—"

"Don't," I said. "Don't ask. I'm too tired even to tell you to go to hell."

"Hard day, huh?" He shook his head sympathetically. "I'll give you a couple bottles when you leave. Anything I can do, keed, anything at all. Just put a name to it."

I sighed and picked up my glass. He was a hard man to say no to, but no was all you could say. Once you said yes, you'd keep right on saying it the rest of your life.

"All right, Stuke," I said. "Let's get back to the beginning. I said I was immune. I can drink your whisky, talk with you, spend an evening with you now and then. I can do you the negative favor of doing nothing. But that's all I can do. That's all

I will do. I will not, as you put it, give you the smallest boost. I will not, either by word or deed, do anything which might even remotely assist in making you county judge."

"Aw, Brownie. Why—?"

"I've told you. You're a menace, a plague, a son-of-a-bitch. You do enough damage where you are, but at least you're bracketed within fairly narrow boundaries. I shudder to think of you operating in the almost unlimited periphery of the judiciary."

"Okay. Throw the big words at me. Show me up. I ain't had no education. I'm just a poor boy who worked hard and—"

"Broth-er!" I said. "When you say that, smile!"

"Well"—he smiled a little sheepishly—"I got an idea how you feel, Brownie. You think a man ought to be a lawyer to—"

"Not necessarily," I said. "The job doesn't require it, and I've known some pretty good judges who weren't lawyers. It could work out, although it violates general precedent, if—*if*, my dear Lem—a man was sincere, honest, and devoted to the public's interest. Which you are not.... No, Stuke, you stay where you are and there'll be no trouble from me. Mr. Lovelace wants the *Courier* all sweetness and light. No scandal, no exposés, nothing that would reflect on the fair name of Pacific City. That's the way he wants it, and that's the way he shall have it—up to a point. You won't be knocked; you won't be blasted out of your present job. But neither will you be boosted upstairs."

He was silent a moment, his black, beady eyes fixed on me in an unblinking stare. Then he shrugged with pretended indifference.

"Suit yourself, Brownie. I was just trying to be a pal to you. The bandwagon's already rolling, and I thought maybe you'd want to hop on."

I choked and coughed. I laughed so hard I almost fell out of my chair. "Stuke. Please!"

"You think I'm lyin', huh?"

"Of course you're lying. When did you ever do anything else?"

"I got plenty of influential friends. How you think I climbed into this job?"

"Like you say," I said, "by working hard. You brought your little red-handled shovel to work with you, and you dug twenty-four hours a day. Before the alarums and excursions were sounded, you had uncovered any number of figurative but exceedingly smelly bodies. Now? Huh-uh. Alas, poor Stuke, they know you well. No more bodies. No county judgeship. No—and I'm probably offending etiquette in mentioning it—whisky in this bottle."

He laughed and popped the cork on another quart. "The whiz don't do anything at all to you, does it, keed? Just makes you spout a little smoother."

"That," I said, "is because I am a *Courier* man. I have my head in the clouds and my feet firmly on the ground."

"Yeah." He grinned. "Ain't it the truth?"

He stopped arguing about the county judge deal. We sat drinking and kidding, listening to the slash of the rain against the windows.

It was only a little after five. Less than an hour ago I'd taken Deborah to the station. But it was almost pitch dark outside with the sudden and violent storm that had struck the city. Stuke shook his black, oily head, cocking a hand to his ear.

"Dig them waves, will you? Almost three blocks away, and you'd think the ocean was coming right through the door."

I nodded absently, thinking of Deborah, wishing I could stop thinking of her. I wondered why she'd said—how she'd known—I was sad, right when I was kidding the hardest.

"What you doing tonight, keed? What you say we step out and play some babes?"

I shook my head. That was an easy one to duck. "Go over to Rose Island tonight? In this storm?"

"Yeah," he sighed, "that's right. No ferries runnin' tonight, and no one would take a charter boat out even if you was crazy enough to ride with 'em.... Maybe I could—"

"Now, Stuke, you should know better than that. No loose women in Pacific City...not in the respectable mainland sections of Pacific City."

"Well—" He broke off abruptly, frowning. He cursed and snapped his fingers. "Christ, pal, I almost forgot to tell you. I ought to have my ass kicked!"

"I'll go along with the last statement," I said. "What about the first one?"

"I'm sorry as hell, keed. I meant to call you at the time, but it was almost three o'clock, see, and I figured you'd already be gone from the office." He swallowed and his eyes shifted away from mine. "She came in on the two-thirty bus, Brownie. One of the boys spotted her."

It was too well done, too carelessly done. Mrs. Clinton Brown's arrival wasn't something that Stuke would forget. By pretending that he had, he was proving the opposite. It meant plenty to him.

"My wife's over on the island?" I said. "I don't suppose you know the address?"

"Well, let's see, now," he frowned. "It's—oh, yeah, it's the

35

Golden Eagle, cottage seven. It ain't so bad as most of 'em, keed. Little tourist camp on the south shore."

"I know what it is," I said. "You can bring your own whore instead of renting theirs."

He clucked his tongue sympathetically. I set my glass down and raised a hand to my temples. I had to do it; I had to cover my face. Sick and stunned as I was, I was choking with laughter.

"It's a damned shame, Brownie. I thought she'd given up bothering you."

"Y-Yeah," I said, shakily. "It's certainly strange."

"How come you put up with her, anyhow? A man's got to support his wife but he don't have to live with her."

"One of those things," I mumbled. I lowered my hand and stood up.

He jumped to his feet also. "Where you going, Brownie? You can't go over to the island tonight. I ain't gonna let you even try it!"

The hell he said! He'd have given his eyeteeth to have me try it.

"Don't worry," I said. "There's no way I could get over there tonight. I just want to go home."

"I'll go with you. I can see this has hit you pretty hard, keed. A time like this, a man needs someone to talk to. I'll take us along a couple bottles, and—"

"I'll take the bottles," I said, "and go by myself."

He looked at me, trying to appear concerned and worried while he sized me up. But there wasn't anything for him to see. The two-way pull had taken hold and he wasn't looking at the real me—the me-in-charge-of-me. I'd moved off to one side, and I was moving faster every second. I was miles away and ahead of him.

"Okay, Brownie," he shrugged, "if that's the way you want it."

He took two quarts of whiskey from a filing cabinet and twisted a newspaper around them. We said good night, and I left.

I walked out to my car, walked not ran, and I was soaked to the skin before I'd gone twenty feet. I slid into the seat, shivering yet not really conscious of the cold. I uncorked one of the bottles and raised it, staring blankly through the streaming windshield.

Until the last time—her last hell-raising visit to Pacific City—I'd been as easy on her as a man could be who was through with his wife. I'd put it to her as I had in the hospital: that it was just simply a case of not loving her any more. But it hadn't worked, and I'd seen it wasn't going to work. In a way, I was actually holding out hope to her. So, the last time, I'd got tough, tough and nasty. And it seemed to have done the job.

She hadn't been in Pacific City for three months. I'd have sworn that in another three months or so she'd be filing for divorce, that she'd make the break final and marry someone else. That was what she would have done. That, I was sure, was what she would have done. Except for Lem Stukey.

Lem wanted something that only I could deliver. He'd been looking for a way to force me to deliver. So I figure he'd started wondering about her, and he'd got in touch with her and started her to wondering: *Think it over, keed. There ain't no other woman; you can't get him to go out with a babe. And the guy's drinkin' himself to death. Something's botherin' him, see? Maybe he done somethin' wrong while he was in the army, and he split with you to keep from mixing you up in it....*

Well, Ellen would know that I hadn't done anything "wrong." She'd know that her Brownie wasn't the kind to commit bigamy or get himself an incurable dose or engage in espionage, or involve himself in any similarly shameful situation or activity. Still, I'd seemed quite contented with our marriage before I entered the army, yet afterward—as soon as I was shipped back to the States—I'd insisted on splitting up. And since there wasn't another woman, since I wasn't in love with someone else, why...?

Stukey had prodded her. He'd kept her mind on the puzzle. And the truth must have finally dawned on her or she wouldn't be here.

It was rather strange, of course, that he'd told me she was back, but—

I shook my head. It wasn't strange. Very little went on in Pacific City that Lem didn't know about. I'd know that he knew she was back, and his failure to tell me would have seemed suspicious. As it was, he hadn't carried the matter off too well. He'd overacted—been a little too offhand. I hadn't thought him capable of embarrassment but obviously he had been.

I held the bottle to my mouth, swallowing steadily. Swallowing and swallowing. A hammer seemed to swing against my heart, numbing it, and another hammer swung against my back, driving through from my back to the heart. And it seemed to push forward, numb and lifeless, and press out through the skin.

Then it slid back into place. The numbness went away. It beat slowly but firmly.

I lowered the bottle. It was more than a third empty. I'd just killed myself, but I wasn't dead. There wasn't, I thought, listening to the roar of the ocean, anything that would kill me. I was going to go right on living, forever and ever, and.... How could I? How could I live in a world of snickers and whisperings and amused pity?

I corked the bottle and started the car.

I drove up to the center of town, circled the Civic Center (WPA 1938), and turned back in the direction I'd come from but on another street. It was probably unnecessary, this maneuvering, but you could never be sure with the Lem Stukeys of the world. They operated with a peculiar shrewdness that transcended intelligence. They had climbed to their pinnacles by doing the unexpected. At any rate, I had plenty of time. Time, with me, was endless.

There was no tail on me; I made sure of the fact. I drove through the wind-hurled downpour to the piers, wound the car through the dark chaos of sheds and warehouses, and parked in the shadows — if shadows there were in this blackness — of a sheet-iron storage building.

I uncorked the bottle and dug some dry cigarettes out of the pocket of the car. I sat drinking and smoking, thinking how strange it was that the thing that had to be done was always the hardest to do.

She wasn't bad, you see. She was weak, spiteful, stubborn; she'd made her own life a hell as a means of making mine one. But, except for what had happened to me, she wouldn't have done what she had. The flaws of character and spirit would never have appeared.

I think the truest maxim ever coined is the one to the effect that untried virtue doesn't count.

Years before, when I was a kid, I owned a little Ford runabout, a Model T. And I took care of that car as a man takes care of his love—for I did love it. I was and remain a Model T guy, more comfortable with imperfection than its opposite, cherishing the ability to discern and shore up a latent weakness. I knew the car wasn't a Cadillac. Hell, what would a guy like me do with a Cad? It was a Model T, and I treated it good and it treated me good. When I sold it, after two years of trouble-free driving, it was actually in better shape than the day I bought it.

Two months later it was on the junk heap.

Less than two months after I split with Ellen, she was whoring.

I belched and kicked open the door of the car. . . . It was too bad but that's the way it was. If I had to live, I had to work. And if I had to work, I had to be around people. And if I had to be around people, I had—I had to be around people. They mustn't know.

Mr. Clinton Brown regrets the necessity of murdering Ellen Tanner Brown.

I stuffed the full bottle into my pocket and carried the other under my arm. I staggered down the pier to the community dock and climbed down the ladder. Somewhere near the foot of it, I paused and peered around in the darkness. Then I said eenie-meenie-miney-moo-toodle-de-doo, and let go.

Everything was a little confused for a moment. My head was planted firmly in a boat, but my feet were in the clouds.

Having great faith in the wisdom of providence, particularly that section dealing with the laws of gravity, I remained unperturbed. *I am a* Courier *man,* I thought, *and a* Courier *man does not miss the boat.*

My feet came down and my head came up, and my ass end was planted firmly in the water. Clear-eyed, I let it remain there while I got the bottle from under my arm and bought myself a drink. Then I pulled it over the side, untied the mooring rope, and picked up the oars.

5

I have never been able to understand the high regard that leaders of dangerous missions have for sobriety. Sober, one challenges the fates; unsober, the fates cannot be bothered with you. While the drunk wanders unharmed amid six-lane traffic, a car swerves up on the sidewalk to pick off the sober man. While the drunk walks away from an eight-story fall, the sober man stumbles from the curb and breaks his neck. It never fails. That's the way it is, so that's the way it is.

Take me, which you are doomed to do for some two hundred pages. Take me. I know nothing about boats. I had never been in a rowboat before. And while I wasn't drunk, naturally, since I cannot get drunk, I was very far from sober. A sober man would never have got fifty feet from the dock. Not being sober, I got a mile and a half, all the way to Rose Island.

Due to my falling or being thrown out of the boat a couple of times, and subsequent willy-nilly driftings while the boat found me again, my trip was something less than speedy. But I got there. I pulled the boat up on the beach and finished the opened bottle. Then, having got my bearings, I headed for the Golden Eagle cottages.

They were only about a block away. I couldn't have debarked

much nearer to them if I'd ridden the ferry and taken a taxi. There were twelve of them, laid out in a triangle with its base to the ocean. Number seven was at the end. Its shades were drawn, but I could detect a little light inside. I seemed to hear a faint stirring and splashing.

I tapped softly on the door. There was silence for a moment, then a splash and a muted, "Yes?"

"Brownie," I said.

"Brownie! What in the—?"

The door flew open. She pulled me inside, stood against me naked, her arms around my neck, her thick black hair buried against my chest.

"Gosh, honey! Gee, it's good to see you! I—but you're soaked! Let me take—"

"I'm all right," I said, and I pushed her away. "I'm going to keep on being all right."

I walked on into the room and sat down in a chair. For a moment she stood where I had pushed her; then she came and sat down on the bed opposite me.

She smiled at me, timidly, swinging her bare legs to and fro, holding her knees together while she swung her legs out from each other. "You're—you're not mad at me, Brownie?"

"I wish you hadn't come back, Ellen," I said. "It's going to make things very hard for both of us."

"No, it won't, honey! I—Did you know I only called the office one time today? Just once! They said you were gone for the day, so I said, thank you. I'll call again tomorrow and—and—that's all I did. Honest!" She nodded her head vigorously, her eyes fixed anxiously on my face.

I said, "So you called one time. Why did you call at all?"

43

"H-Haven't you any idea, Brownie?"

"Sure. You had a dime."

The smile faded and a sullen look edged into its place. Then the look faded, without disappearing, and the smile—a semblance of it—returned. "Maybe...I guess maybe you've got a right to talk that way. But—but think of me, honey! I h-hadn't done anything, and—"

"Hadn't done anything!" I jeered. "You didn't need to do anything. I didn't know my way around when I married you. I'd never been anywhere or seen anything. After I did, I wised up. I saw I was married to a goddamned flabby-tailed dumbbell with a fried egg for a brain."

"You dirty bas—! Oh, Brownie, *don't!* Don't, honey. You don't mean—"

"The hell I don't! I've seen better tail on a mule."

She stuttered and spluttered, trying to curse and beg me at the same time. Trying to fight down her temper. I'd touched her on her sore spots. She *didn't* have much in the way of an education. Her rear end *was* a little on the wriggly side.

"Y-You burn me up! You—"

"Not me," I said, "that hot little business of yours. Remember that poem I dedicated to you?"

"You're goddamned right, I remember! Of all the dirty—"

"By the way, what did you do with the rest of those sonnets? I was thinking, perhaps, you'd like to have them autographed."

She told me what she'd done with them. Something indelicate but completely practical.

"They didn't catch fire?"

"You burn me—That's right! Sit there and laugh! You done—you did all this! Why shouldn't you laugh about it?"

44

"Jesus," I said. "What a freak you turned out to be! Do the boys make you put a sack over your head?"

It was going swell. She was getting angrier and angrier. I had her sold, and if I could just keep her that way...she'd live.

I—

She began to cry.

She'd very seldom done that, really cried. She'd grown up in pretty rugged circumstances, and she'd never got the crying habit. But on those rare occasions when she did break down, she pulled all the stops. She cried like the child she'd never been.

She didn't cover her face with her hands, and all of it was puckered and reddened. Her eyes were tight shut. Her nose ran. Her mouth, with the ludicrously drawn-down corners, opened so wide you could see her tonsils.

I tried to laugh, and I couldn't. I jerked the cork on the second quart and took a big slug, and it didn't do any good. It had always got me to see her cry. It did now.

You do not have your head in the clouds, Brown, I thought. *Your feet are of clay and the arches are falling.*

I took another drink. I gripped the arms of the chair. I said, "Look, now. Now see here, dammit. There's no sense in — in —"

And she shuddered and sobbed. "Y-You — you h-hurt my f-feelings...."

And suddenly I was on the bed with her, dabbing at her eyes with my handkerchief, telling her to blow her nose, dammit. And she shuddered and choked back the tears.

"Aw r-right, Brownie. I — I — w-will."

She clung to me, shivering with my wetness but clinging tighter when I tried to draw away. She curled up on the bed, drawing me down with her, burrowing and snuggling her head against my shoulder.

After a while, she said, "H-Honey...?"

"Yes," I said.

Another silence. Then: "I know what—what happened. I don't know why I didn't guess in the beginning, because you couldn't be mean to anyone and—"

"All right," I said. "You know."

"Why didn't you tell me, honey? It wouldn't have made any difference. There's more to marriage than—than *that*."

"A great deal more," I said. "There's more to a house than a roof, but you'd find it impractical to live without one. You'd move from one room to another and they'd all be fine—and not worth a damn. Finally, you'd have to move out."

"You don't know! You can't be sure! It—you think this is better?"

"It doesn't need to be like this. I hoped you'd remarry."

"I can't! H-How can I when I still love you?"

My hands trembled on her bare back. I had to keep on, but I knew it was no use. She was a child, weeping for a broken doll, stubbornly refusing any other.

"Look," I said. "Listen to me, Ellen. A lot of people have thought I was a pretty smart guy. You always thought so. Have you changed your mind?"

"No, Brownie, but—"

"Wasn't I always good to you? Didn't I always do what was best for you? Now, answer me. Isn't that so?"

"Yes."

"Why do you think I did it this way? Do you think it was easy for me, ridiculing you, breaking every bond between us so that you could form new ones with someone else? Do you think it's something that popped into my mind on the spur of the moment?"

"Of course not, honey. But—"

"I thought it over for weeks. I studied the record of what had happened in similar cases. I talked it over with two damned good psychiatrists. I told them what you—we—were like, and—"

Her head jerked back. "Like? What *am* I supposed to be like?"

"Don't," I said. "Let's not get started on another row. I told them the truth, that you were anything but a nympho but also very far from frigid. I told them that you'd always—Well, skip it. There wasn't any real best thing to do, but I did the best there was."

"And look how it turned out!"

"It would have turned out this way anyhow, if you can't face facts. My telling you the truth wouldn't have made any difference. Don't you—"

"We could have tried, couldn't we? How do you know how it would have turned out when we didn't even try? You don't know everything! You. . . . Oh"—she hesitated and I heard her swallow heavily—"it's—it's t-too late, Brownie? You don't want to come back to me now, after what I've—I've—?"

I kissed her on the forehead, wondering abstractedly why the weakest of us seem always subjected to the greatest stress. Good and evil: were there such things or were there only weakness and strength? Was a car bad because it became junk? Was a woman bad who became a whore?

"Brownie . . . is th-that the reason why—?"

47

I kissed her again. "You haven't done anything," I said. "Not a single thing."

"Let's try it, Brownie! Why, honestly, I won't mind a bit! Really, I won't. We'll have all those nice funny talks together, and you can read to me in the evenings and—and maybe we can get Skipper back from those people! Or we can get another dog. Why, we could even adopt a baby, honey, and it would be just like—"

"Don't," I said. "For Christ's sake, DON'T!"

But she wouldn't stop. She went on and on, over and over, that one refrain, earnest, tearful, laughable, maddening: *It wouldn't, honey! It wouldn't make a bit of difference!* My heart began to beat time to it. The blood roared and raced through my brain, beating time.

"Brownie!" she said. "Brownie!"

I drifted back from a faraway place. A place where all the straight paths were blocked off and everything moved at a tangent.

Her voice had become firm. "You understand, Brownie! We're stopping this foolishness right now! We need each other, and we're going to have each other. I've tried your way. Now you're going to try mine. I'm going to—I'm going to make you, Brownie!"

"Spread it all out," I said. "Lay the cards down."

"I—cards?"

"Card, then. Lem Stukey. Either I do as you say, or you get tough. You get me or you have a little talk with Lem."

She drew her head back, looked into my face, frowning. "I d-don't understand. What would I—?"

"He's been in touch with you, hasn't he? He sent you the dough to come back here on?"

"We-ell, he—he—" She blushed. "Well, he was just being nice. Just because he liked me."

I laughed.

"Well, he was—he does!" she snapped. "What's so funny about it?"

"Nothing," I said. "But that's the deal, isn't it, El? You have to tell me, you know. You can't make threats without showing what you're threatening."

"But I haven't—" She paused; she was silent for several seconds. "What if I—how could I threaten you with *that?*" she said, in a half-shamed voice. "It isn't any crime. You couldn't help—"

"You know what I mean," I said. "You know what I'm like. You know what the newspaper business is like. It's a closed world; there's no place you can go where you're not known. Put it in plain language. Put yourself in my place. How long could you live in a world where everyone knew you didn't have a pecker?"

"Brownie! That's dir—"

"You mean it's funny," I said. "Sure it is. You could even catch the doctors and nurses in the hospital grinning about it. You know I couldn't take it, El. You may not know that I might not get the chance to take it. Because there are a hell of a lot of places that wouldn't hire me. That's right; that's straight from the case histories. They're afraid of you. They figure you're not normal."

"But—listen to me, Brownie! I—"

"That's what you're threatening me with," I said. "You'd do that to me, or you'd let Lem do it. Put me under his thumb for keeps. You'd take away the only thing I have left, the little pride and integrity that gives me an excuse to go on living. You love me—you can't love anyone else, you say—and you'd do that to me?"

"*No!*" She gripped me fiercely. "No, I won't, Brownie, I won't have to because—No, I won't do it, honey! I didn't know what I was thinking about! I've just been kind of crazy and lonely and hopeless-feeling, and—" Her voice trailed off.

After a moment she said reproachfully, a trifle angrily, "After all, I *could* get a divorce on those grounds. That would be a lot worse, wouldn't it?"

You see? She didn't know what she was going to do. How, then, could I?

"Yes," I said. "That would be worse. You wouldn't get the nice chunk of change you can get out of Lem."

"I—You've got a lot of right to talk about him," she said, "after the way you've acted. You're the one that's always running people down. Even if I did tell him, what makes you think he'd—"

"For God's sake!" I said. "What are you saying, Ellen? First, you don't have anything to threaten me with. Next, you have something but you're not going to use it. Then, you're going to use it—you're going to pass it on to Lem—but he isn't going to. You don't make sense from one minute to—"

"Oh, sure!" she said sullenly. "You're a genius, and I'm a dumbbell. Well, maybe I'm not as dumb as you think."

"Let it go. It's no use," I said.

"Whatever I got out of Stukey it wouldn't be enough! After all I've been through!"

"No," I said. "It wouldn't be enough."

I sat up and uncorked the bottle. I took a drink, replaced the cork, and fumbled for a cigarette. I didn't have any with me, of course, any dry ones. They were back in the car. I reached out to the reading stand, took a cigarette from her package, and lighted it.

"Brownie—" She sat up, too, half sat up, with her legs folded under her.

"Yes?" I said.

"You know I wouldn't do that, don't you?" She smiled at me brightly. "It's like you say. How could I when I love you so much? And—but, oh, Brownie! Let's go back together! Please, darling. It won't make any difference, and even if it does a little it'll still be better than this. I just can't go on like—"

"No," I said. "You can't, and you won't."

And I brought the bottle down on her head.

I stood looking down at her, and my head swam and I weaved slowly on my feet. The wetness and the exertion and the long talk were sobering me, and when I sobered I became drunk. Far drunker than any amount of whisky could make me. All my sureness was gone, and the ten thousand parts of an insane puzzle were scattered to the winds.

She lay, twitching a bit and moaning, with her head and shoulders slumping toward her knees, her thighs in a tangent curve to her legs. A question mark. She was a question, and she had to be answered.

Had it been necessary?

Or had I done it because I wanted to?

Was every move I made, as Dave Randall had once angrily declared, designed to extract payment from the world for the hell I dwelt in? Had I tried to destroy slowly and, failing that, killed wantonly?

It was a nice question. It was something to think about on these long rainy evenings.

I took another stiff drink.

The terrible sobriety-drunkenness, with its terrible questions, began to fade. I slid back into the sideways world. This was the way it was, and the way it was was this.

Yet it was hard to leave her like this. Something seemed to need doing, some small thing. Something she'd always wanted, perhaps, without conscious awareness of the want.

I could think of only one thing.

I pulled the sheet over her now semi-conscious body. I upended the bottle of whisky and sprinkled it over the sheet. I jerked several matches from a pad and struck them.

"You said to," I said. "Remember, Ellen? You always said to burn you up. . . ."

And I let the matches fall.

6

It was still pitch dark outside, still raining a downpour, but the wind was dying and the worst of the storm seemed to be over. I pushed the boat into the bay and hopped in. I started to row. And then, slowly, I let the oars slide out of my hands and drift away into the darkness.... Let the boat decide, I thought. Leave it to the ocean. They brought me here; now, they can return me. Or not return me. I wash my hands of all responsibility.

I leaned back across the thwarts, letting my fingers trail in the water. I closed my eyes, feeling the boat rock and roll, feeling it turn round and round gently as it moved out into the bay. It was very peaceful for a time. Very restful. I had had nothing to do with anything, and now I had nothing to do with this. I was a man following orders, clear-eyed, clear-thinking, and if those orders had led me—led me...

She had looked very beautiful. She had glowed, oh, but definitely she had glowed. She had been all lit up, burning with a clear-blue flame, and then the mattress had started to smolder and...

I screamed but there was no sound. I was throwing up.

The boat had begun to spin. It was caught in the trough between two tall shore-bound rollers, pulled by one and pushed by the other, and it spun faster and faster. Suddenly it reared up on end and shot to the crest of the first wave. It hung poised there for a moment, then it dropped down, spinning, to the other side.

Tons of water plunged into it. It went down, vanished as completely as though it had never existed, and I went on. There was a thunderous roar, an incessant crashing. And then I was gripping something hard and slimy...one of the piles of the pier.

That's the way it was to be, then. The decision had been made. I pulled myself from pile to pile until I found the ladder. I climbed up to the pier and returned to my car. I drove away.

My house—to use the noun loosely—is some six miles north of Pacific City. Years ago it was occupied by a railroad section gang—in the days when section hands were largely itinerant Mexicans. When I discovered it, it was a lopsided ruin, headquarters seemingly for the county's population of creeping and crawling things.

The railroad gladly rented it to me for five dollars a month. A hundred dollars and a few hundred hours' work had made it reasonably habitable. It is a little noisy, perhaps, since it sits on railroad right-of-way, and it is more than a little sooty. But as rental properties go in Pacific City—properties within the financial reach of the modest-salaried man—it is still very much a bargain. We do not believe in "government handouts" here, you see. We scorn socialistic housing programs. We hold to the American way of life, the good old laws of supply and demand. That is, the landlords supply what they care to in the way of housing and demand what they feel like. And the tenant, bless him, oh, hail his rugged independence, is perfectly free to pay it and like it. Or sleep in the streets. Where, of course, he will be promptly arrested by Lem Stukey for vagrancy.

I will say this for Stukey: he is absolutely fearless and relentless where vagrants are concerned. Let Lem and his minions apprehend some penniless wanderer, preferably colored and over sixty-five, and the machinery of the law goes into swift and remorseless action. Sixty days on the road gang, six months on the county farm—so it goes. Nor is that always as far as it goes. In an amazing number of instances, the vagrant appears to be the very person responsible for a long series of hitherto unsolved crimes....

Good old Lem and his rubber hose! Unless I missed my guess, I'd be seeing him shortly.

I parked my car at the side of the house and went inside. I filled a water glass with whisky and put it down at a gulp. Fire blazed through me. My heart did frantic setting-up exercises for a moment, then steadied off into a slow, steady pounding. All at once I felt almost happy. For the first time in a long time, life seemed really interesting. There was a rift—and a widening one—in the dead-gray monotony of existence.

I went into the bedroom and shucked out of my clothes. The phone rang and I trotted back into the living-room to answer it, pulling a robe around me.

"Brownie—Clint?" It was Dave Randall.

"Why, Colonel," I said. "How nice of you to call! How are all the wee ones and—"

"Brownie, for God's sake! Have you seen Lem Stukey?"

"Frequently," I said. "As a devoted *Courier* man, I am brought into contact with many strange—"

"Please, Brownie! He hasn't been in touch with you in the last hour or so?"

"No"—I put a frown into my voice—"what's up, Dave?"

"It's about—Where have you been all evening, Clint? Lem's been tearing up the town to find you. He called me. He even called Mr. Lovelace."

"But why? What about?"

I smiled to myself. It was wonderful to be interested again.

"I—I think I'd better come out there, Brownie. I think, perhaps, I'd better bring Mr. Lovelace with me."

"Oh?" I said, and I made the voice-frown a little stronger. "What's the trouble, Dave?"

"I can't—I think I'd better tell you in person. Brownie—"

"Yes?"

"Where have you been tonight?"

"Drinking. Riding and drinking. Walking and drinking. Sitting by the roadside and drinking."

"Were you with anyone? Is there any way you could establish your whereabouts?"

"No," I said, "to both questions.... Look, Dave, I didn't run over anyone, did I? I was pretty woozy, but—"

"I'll see you," he said. "I'll be right out."

We hung up. I sat down on the lounge and went to work on the bottle. I was feeling better and better. There was nothing in my stomach but this clean, fresh whisky, and there was nothing in my mind but a problem. No Ellen. No oblong of bright-blue flame. Only an interesting problem.

About ten minutes had passed when a car roared up the lane from the highway and skidded to a stop in the yard. It was Lem Stukey, and he was by himself. Naturally, on anything as good as this, he would be by himself. I looked up as he walked in. I blinked my eyes, frowned, and took another drink from the bottle.

He stood in the doorway, his hands on his hips, his hat thrust back on his oily head. And there was an expression of sad reproach on his sleek, round face.

He waited for me to speak. I let him go right on waiting. Finally he crossed the room and pulled up a chair in front of me.

"Keed," he said, sorrowfully, "you shouldn't've done it. You should have knowed you couldn't get away with it."

"Well," I shrugged, "nothing ventured, nothing gained."

"She wasn't worth it, Brownie."

"No," I said, "I don't suppose she was. But, then, who is?"

"I don't see no way out for you, keed. Not unless I was to kind of take a hand personally. If I was to do that, now, call it an accident—"

"Why don't you?" I said. "After all, a pal's a pal, I always say."

"You mean that, Brownie? You'll play ball with me like I been askin' you to?"

"Well"—I hesitated—"isn't it pretty muddy outside?"

"Muddy? I don't dig you, keed."

"To play ball."

"Look!" he snarled, and his hand closed over my arm. "What the hell are you talking about?"

"I don't know," I said. "What are you talking about?"

He jumped up and stood over me. I started to rise and he shoved me back hard.

"I'm talking about murder, you smart bastard! You were over to the island tonight. You killed her. You cold-cocked her and set fire to her. Left her to burn up in the bed. Only she didn't burn up, see. She didn't die right away. I figure her hair probably cushioned the blow, and she came to when she felt herself burnin'. Anyway, she got up and got to the dresser. She got something out of her purse. She had it balled up in her hand when the island cops found her."

I looked at him, blinking a little owlishly, sifting through the situation one fact at a time. It wasn't particularly startling, although I suspect that I was guilty of at least a small start. I'd been pretty wobbly on my pins when I swung the bottle, and she did have a thick head of hair. And the whisky would have tended to burn away before the bedclothes themselves caught fire.

Now, as to this "something" she'd taken from her purse...

"To borrow an expression," I said, "I don't dig you, keed. Just who am I supposed to have killed?"

"Don't pull that innocent crap on me! Who the hell else would have killed your wife? She wasn't robbed. It's a cinch it wasn't a rape murder. Anyone that wanted any of that could have had it for—"

I came up then, and I came up swinging. I hit him an open-palmed slap across the jaw, hit him so hard his hat sailed from his head. His hand darted to his hip, but he didn't draw the gun. I sat back down again and buried my face in my hands.

After a while I said, "Are you sure it was murder? It couldn't have been an accident?"

"Who you kidding?" he said. "You goin' to tell me that she fell on *top* of her head? That she wiped the place clean of fingerprints herself?"

"Wi—!" I caught myself, choked the word into a meaningless grunt. "This object she had in her hand. What was it?"

"A poem, kind of a poem. She put the finger right on you, keed. She'd had it a long time; it was practically worn out with all the folding and refolding it had gone through. You wrote it for her, and she'd been carrying it around all this time. Ever since you split up. Yessir, she knew that when we saw it, we'd—"

"It had my name on it?"

"It didn't need no name on it. She never really went for no one but you. Anyway, she sure wasn't going for anyone three–four years ago when this must've been written. When you an' her were still tied up."

"Maybe she wrote it herself."

"Huh-uh. She wasn't up to anything that sharp. And what the hell? A dame's dying, and she goes for a poem she's written? You know better than that, keed. You wrote it. It sounds like you to a *t*, and she knew I'd see that—"

"What was it?" I said. "Have you got it with you?"

"It figures, Brownie. It all adds up to just one guy. No one else had any motive. No one else would have written a thing like this. It had to be someone that lives here—someone I'd know—and, palsy, that ain't no one but—"

"I'd like to hear it," I said. "Do you mind?"

"I don't mind a bit, keed." He took a notebook from his pocket and opened it. "Catch a load. I don't know that I can pronounce all the words just right, but—"

"Go ahead. I'll try to interpret."

"Sure," he said, and he read:

> *Lady of the endless lust,*
> *Itching lips and heaving bust,*
> *Lady save it, lady scram, lady hang it on a nail*
> *Get thee hence nor leave behind you*
> *Any vestige of your tail.*

He finished reading and looked at me sharply. I looked back at him indifferently. I'd written it, of course, it and some fifty or sixty similar bits of doggerel. But that had been long ago, and they'd been done on various odds and ends of paper and on a variety of typewriters. On the Red Cross machines in hospitals. In newspaper offices. In dollar-an-hour, type-your-own-letter places. They couldn't be traced to me. I'd written them out of bitterness and brooding—at a time when I was still bitter and brooding—out of hate and resentment and restlessness. And, finally, I had presented them to Ellen. I had dedicated them to her.

I'd shown them to no one but her. No one but she knew that I had written them. I wondered what masochistic urge had led her to save this one after destroying the others.

"Well, keed?" Stukey grinned at me. "What you say?"

"I gather that that's a copy," I said. "Where's the original?"

"The cops over on the island have it. They read it off to me over the telephone."

"You haven't seen it yourself, then? You don't actually know that it's as they described it? Old and creased and—"

"What the hell you gettin' at?"

"I've already arrived. But you, my dear Stukey, are very far behind. You didn't see the poem. You didn't see her. You don't know—"

"They're kidding me, huh?" He let out a snort. "They made it all up just to cause some excitement."

"You're chief of detectives. You seem to regard this as a pretty important case. So important that you had to bother my publisher and editor about it. Yet you've got your evidence by telephone. Why? Why didn't you go over there?"

"Well—uh—" He licked his lips. "You know, keed. The bay's been kinda choppy. Ain't no real reason why I couldn't have gone, if I'd figured it was necessary, but—uh—"

"A little choppy, eh? The ferries and charter boats aren't running, and it's just a little choppy. Cut it out, Stuke. You didn't go because you couldn't. No one could have."

"That's what you say! I—"

"So did you, earlier this evening. Remember our conversation at your office? No one could have crossed that bay tonight. *No one.* Certainly he couldn't have crossed it twice. If you don't know that, you ought to be back walking a beat, which, now that I think of it, might be an excellent idea."

His face reddened; his round, overbright little eyes shifted nervously. "Now, look, Brownie. It's just as plain as day—"

"—or the nose on your face." I nodded. "But you can't see it. You were so red hot to get something on me that you overlooked the plain facts of the matter. You say that she got up and got that poem out of her purse. How do you know she did? How do you know it wasn't simply made to look that way by the person who killed her?"

"Well—" His tongue moved over his lips again. "But why would—?"

"The poem belonged to him, the murderer, not her. Obviously he was a man with a perverted sense of humor, a maniac in the broad sense of the term. He visited her, doubtless as a client. He murdered her. Then he arranged for her to be found in such a way as to throw you off his trail yet satisfy his ego. And, stupid man that you are, he was entirely successful."

I smiled at him pleasantly and took another drink. I lighted a cigarette, coughing slightly on the smoke as I choked back a laugh. This was far better than I had thought it would be. There were truly wonderful possibilities in it.

"That's what happened, Lem," I said. "It had to be a maniac. You can't make sense out of it in any other way."

"You call that sense?" he growled.

"For a maniac, a sadistic killer, yes. By the way, I assume the ferries have resumed service? Well, then, you've let him get completely away from you. He's not even on the island any more."

There was something very close to fear in the too-bright eyes. Fear and wonder and awe. "You're"—he cleared his throat hoarsely—"you're takin' it pretty calm, keed. Your wife gets killed in just about the most God-awful way a woman could, and you sit there grinning and—"

"She wasn't my wife," I said. "She hadn't been my wife in a long, long time. As for my reaction to the—the—well, I don't wear my emotions on my sleeve, Stuke. My actions don't necessarily reflect my feelings."

"Yeah," he grunted. "I'll buy that. I'll go right on down the line on that one. I sit listenin' to you sometimes, chewin' the fat with you, and I get to wonderin' what the hell—"

I held up a hand, interrupting him. "I'll tell you what you'd better do, Stuke. What you'd better start wondering about. You've botched this thing from beginning to end. My wife has been brutally murdered by a maniac, and you've let him get away. You'd better start wondering about how you're going to keep your job."

"I had, huh?" He laughed nervously. "Now, look, Brownie, like I said a moment ago, she just wasn't worth any bad trouble."

"I disagree with you.... What did you say when you talked to

Dave Randall and Mr. Lovelace tonight? Something rather suggestive, eh, laden with nasty implications?"

"Me? Me knock a pal?" He made a gesture of hurt denial. "You know I wouldn't do a thing like that. All I done was mention that your wife had been killed, an' that I—well, I was trying to get ahold of you to break the bad news. That's all I said, Brownie. So help me."

I shrugged. I didn't particularly care what he'd said. I still wasn't letting him off the hook. Mr. Lem Stukey was going to go to work, at long last. He was going to give the city a long-delayed cleaning up. Not strictly because of the entertainment it would provide me, not entirely. Through him I could make atonement. I could offset with good the evil of Ellen's death.

"I'm telling you, Brownie," he said, "I didn't knock you. There ain't nothin' for either of us to get in an uproar about. Now, I been thinkin', and the way I see it we're both off base. It was an accident."

"It couldn't have been. You said so yourself."

"I can't change my mind? An accident's got to be logical? She was drinking. She spilled booze all over herself. She catches herself on fire, lighting a cigarette. She falls down and knocks herself out. She—"

"Before or after igniting herself? And what about the poem?"

"Look, Brownie"—he leaned forward, pleading—"we get cases like this all the time. Just about like this. Someone gets stiff in his hotel room. He bangs himself up an' flops down on the bed smoking, and he wakes up burning an' the room's so full of smoke he can't see. An'—well, you know how it is. He tries to get out of the place, but he wants to take his money with him, so—"

"I see." I nodded slowly. "You think that's what she intended to do, huh? She tried to get her money, but got the poem instead. Mmm, I suppose it might have been that way. But that still doesn't explain the poem."

"What's there to explain? Lots of people carry poems around. We got a fellow down at the office—you know him, Stengel, works over in identification—and he does it. He clips 'em out of newspapers, or maybe he hears 'em over the radio and copies 'em down. Never seen him yet when he didn't have some verse in his wallet, ready to spring it on you."

"But this particular little item—"

"Look, Brownie, pal"—his eyes flickered with annoyance—"you're fighting me. It was pretty cute, wasn't it? Something a dame like—something she might have got a big bang out of. Maybe she copied it off a privy wall. Maybe some place where she was working, slingin' hash, say, and one of the waitresses passed it around and she got hold of a copy. The point is it don't mean nothing, so we don't even have to consider it. I ain't even going to mention it in my report."

"Well—" I stared at him absently.

"Well?" he said. "It was an accident, huh? We let it go at that. I don't give you no trouble; you don't give me none."

I hesitated. I was trying to remember something. Everything was reasonably clear up to a certain point: I could remember swinging the bottle, spilling the whisky over her, dropping the matches. But after that...

After that, from that time until I reached the boat, nothing. Only the long blue oblong of flame, and then nothing. If Stukey hadn't been so sure of himself, if he hadn't gone off half-cocked, he might have tripped me up in a dozen places.

"You were very sure," I said, "that she'd been slugged. There wasn't any doubt in your mind. What made you so certain, Stuke? Just the fact that she couldn't have easily struck the top of her head against something?"

"That was a big part of it, sure, but there was this quart whisky bottle layin' in the bed an'—"

"I see. You thought she'd been hit with that. What brand of whisky was it?"

"Couldn't say. It was all charred, see, the label burned off and—"

"And the fingerprints? Did you dust the place?"

"Uh-huh. The boys went over it from top to bottom, and the only prints they found was hers an' a few of the maid's. I figure she must've cleaned the place up good before she started her party. Nice clean little lady, huh?" He drooped a lid over one eye. "Looks like she even wiped off the doorknob."

"I suppose the boys also looked for tracks around the outside?"

"Tracks? Why, keed, there could have been a herd of elephants around that place and their tracks wouldn't have lasted five minutes in that rain."

"Now, that poem—"

"Forget it. Put it out of your mind, pal. Typewritten—God knows when or where. The paper, it might have come from any-place. A dime store or a drugstore or—"

"You were completely wrong then in your initial suspicions? There is absolutely nothing to connect me with this murder?"

"Absitively and possolutely, Brownie. I was all wet up to here. But don't use that word, huh? Don't say murder. It was an accident and—"

A car was pulling into the yard. He paused, shooting me a look of inquiry.

"That would be my publisher," I said, "and my editor. They have come to condole with me. Also, I suspect—at least on the part of Mr. Randall—to lend me moral support."

"Yeah? Well, that's nice." He stood up, brushing at his pants. "I guess I'll just trot along, then, an'—"

"You," I said, "will stay right here."

"But, pal...Oh, well, sure. You want me to square you up with 'em, huh? I don't remember saying anything out of the way, but—"

"You will square yourself up," I said. "You will explain just what you intend to do about apprehending my wife's murderer."

7

Mr. Lovelace was patently not in the most pleasant of humors. A man of regular habits was Mr. Lovelace, a man who, like so many of the lower lower-animals, liked his full ten hours' sleep each night. Now that sleep had been disturbed; he, Austin Lovelace, had been disturbed twice in *one* night! And without, as he saw it, any very adequate cause.

It was the old, old story. Because he was strong and wise—a tower of strength among pygmies—he was constantly overburdened. Everyone loaded his trifling troubles upon him.

He was sleepy, puzzled, fretful. Very, very fretful. For me, the loyal, hard-working—and appreciative—servant, he managed a mumbled word of sympathy and a semi-fatherly handclasp. But it was obviously an effort.

"Very sad. Tragic....Insist you take the remainder of the week off, understand? Take as much time as you need—uh—within reason."

"Thank you, sir," I said. "I believe two or three days will be sufficient. I own a burial plot in Los Angeles, and I thought—"

"By all means. Certainly. Much better than a local burial. Incidentally, Mr. Brown"—his lips pursed pettishly—"I was rather shocked to learn that—uh—that a man of your caliber was married to—to—"

"I understand, sir," I said. "But I was very young at the time. It was long before I came to the *Courier*. I hadn't yet had the chance to profit from my association with you."

"Well—ahem—I, uh, certainly wouldn't want to chide you in your hour of bereavement. Am I correct in understanding that you had not lived together as man and wife for some time?"

"Not for several years, sir. Not since I entered the army."

"Ummm. I see." The stare he gave me was considerably less peevish. "A marriage in name only, eh? A youthful mistake from which you were unable to extricate yourself?"

"Yes, sir," I said. "You might call it that."

It was bad, shameful, to speak of her in this way. But, you see, there no longer was a her. Now there was merely a problem, and out of the bad much good could come.

He gave me a forgiving clap on the back. Then, after a look of puzzled distaste at Lem Stukey, he turned annoyed to Dave Randall.

"Well, Randall? I believe there's nothing more to be said or done, eh?"

"N-No, sir." Dave started nervously. "I—I guess it wasn't necessary for you to—I guess I shouldn't have bothered you to come out here, sir."

"My own thought. Why did you, Randall? I seem to recall that you mentioned that you would later explain the need for my presence."

"Well, I—I—"

"Yes? Speak up, man!"

Lovelace fed on nervousness, even as he did on flattery. Let him catch you jumpy, uneasy, and he would be after you like a hungry hound. And Dave couldn't explain, of course. He couldn't say what he'd thought — that he was sure I was in a bad hole and was apt to need plenty of help to climb out.

He'd been positively pale with fear when he arrived, and he'd been almost pitifully relieved when it dawned on him that I was very far from the shadows of the gas chamber. That was all he could think of: that I wasn't guilty; that what he had done to me, through a serious error in judgment when he was my commanding officer, had not resulted in murder.

Now he had to think of something else. The old man was demanding an explanation. And Dave could only stand and squirm, stammer helplessly.

"Mr. Randall! Are you keeping something from me?"

"N-No, sir. I — I guess I was just a little excited, sir."

"Yes? I would not have said that you were an excitable type, Mr. Randall. Are you — uh — are the duties of your position too much for you? Would you like to step down for a time?"

I decided to intervene. Not, you understand, that I greatly minded Dave's squirming. The good colonel — he who had been so cocksure, so peremptory with his orders — would do much more squirming before I was finished with him. I intervened because it suited me. It was time to start taking the good from the bad.

"I believe I can explain, sir," I said. "We'll want the story for our first edition. I imagine Dave thought we'd better discuss the handling of it."

"Oh? Well, why didn't he say so, then? No reason to — *Story!*" He gulped, his eyes widening in a horrified double-take. "Did you say story, Mr. Brown? Surely, you don't plan on —"

"We'll have to, sir. This is one we won't be able to bury. It's another Black Dahlia case. The Los Angeles papers will give it a whopping play. It'll be a front-page story in every paper between here and L.A. We couldn't pass it up, even if we wanted to."

"*If* we wanted to? *If,* Mr. Brown? You know the policy of the *Courier.* A family paper for family people."

"If," I repeated, and Lem Stukey cleared his throat.

"Them other papers," he said. "They won't play up the story if there ain't one. We keep quiet about it here—call it an accident—and what are they gonna—"

"But it wasn't an accident," I said. "It was murder. And knowing Mr. Lovelace as I do, I feel certain that he will not blink at it. He will not hush it up, and thus leave unchanged the conditions that gave rise to the crime."

Lovelace's jaw sagged. Slowly he sank down on the lounge.

"I'm sorry, sir," I said. "I'm sure you must see that I am right."

"B-But the *Courier*...Pacific City! I just—Uh, what did you mean, Brown? About the conditions which gave rise to it?"

I didn't answer immediately. I poured a drink and pressed the glass into his hand, and he took it like a child taking candy. He swigged it, shuddered, and swigged again. I sat down and began talking.

Stukey scowled down at the floor. Dave listened, watching me curiously, but nodding occasionally at what I said.

"...a very unhealthy situation here for some time, Mr. Lovelace. The sort of situation that breeds murder. Riffraff drifting in from everywhere because of the climate. Thieves, pickpockets, prostitutes, confidence workers. Keep that—them—in mind, and then bear in mind that we have a large floating tourist population, people with money and—"

"But—but I don't understand!" Lovelace frowned querulously at Lem. "Why have you allowed this, sir? Weren't you aware of these undesirables in our midst? What kind of chief of detectives do you call yourself?"

"As a matter of fact," I said, carefully, "Mr. Stukey has kept them under quite good control. But he's only one man, not the entire department. And I think we've made his job seem a pretty thankless one. There's been little or no recognition for work well done. There's been no incentive to give the city the wholesale housecleaning it needs."

"Incentive? Recognition?" He continued to frown at Stukey. "He draws a very handsome salary, as I recall. Why should he—?"

"Don't we all, sir? Don't we all need more than mere money? For that matter, we've had something worse here than a lack of incentive. There's not only been no encouragement to do something about local crime, there's been every encouragement to do nothing. I think you know what I mean, sir. You're sensitive about the good name of Pacific City. The police department knows it, as do we all. Naturally, the tendency has been to keep the lid on crime rather than to expose it and cast it out."

He didn't like that. Mr. Lovelace, need it be said, liked no criticism, either implied or direct. So, after letting him hang for a moment, I lifted him off the hook.

"Of course, I'm not excusing Mr. Stukey. In the final analysis, the fault is largely if not completely his. He chose the easy way out, the course of least resistance. After all, sir, it hasn't been exactly pleasant for me to lay these facts before you. But I felt that it was my duty to do it—I did not see how I could delay longer in view of tonight's happenings—and I knew that you, sir, regardless of your personal feelings, have nothing but respect and admiration for the man who does his duty."

He puffed up a little. Some of the sag went out of his shoulders. "Quite right, Mr. Brown. And—uh—thank you for the compliment. I hope, naturally, that the situation is not as bad as you believe.... What do you recommend?"

"Solving this murder," I said, "should be the first item on our agenda. At least, we should leave no stone unturned in trying to solve it. We want to serve notice to the world at large that murder is not taken lightly in Pacific City."

He sighed, hesitated, nodded firmly. "Yes, yes. By all means.... You, sir—Stukey, is it? What are you doing about this murder?"

"What murder?" Lem grunted, sullenly. "He says it's murder. I don't."

"How's that? Mr. Brown—?"

"Mr. Stukey is a conservative," I said. "He's jumped to the wrong conclusions a time or two and it's made him ultra cautious. I wish it were an accident, sir, but I'm sure you'll agree with me that it couldn't have been...."

I explained the circumstances under which the body had been found, bearing down heavily on the wiped-away fingerprints. He nodded grimly, scowling at Stukey.

"Certainly it was murder, some mentally deranged person.... You don't agree, sir? You intend to persist in your quaint theory that—"

"I ain't overlooking any bets," said Lem, hastily. "I got the island boys workin' on the murder angle. I thought maybe— maybe I might have a line on the killer myself, but...but I'll keep 'em on it, Mr. Lovelace. We'll turn that place upside down."

"Well, I should think so!" snapped Lovelace. "An accident! Whatever led you to think for a moment that—?"

"I was just tryin' to keep an open mind, Mr. Lovelace." Stukey was almost whining. "Like I said, I ain't passing up any bets."

Lovelace harrumphed angrily and glanced at me. I said I had complete confidence in Mr. Stukey's ability to handle the case. "I'm not sure that he needs or wants any suggestions from me, but—"

"Certainly he does! Why shouldn't he?"

"Well," I went on, "it seems to me that the two things tie in together—that is, the solving of the murder and the city-wide clean-up. I believe that every known or suspected criminal, every person who has no legitimate reason for his presence here, should be brought in and questioned. Probably the murderer will be among them. If not—well, we will have done our best. At any rate, as rapidly as the suspects are eliminated, they should be ordered out of the city and kept out."

"Excellent," said Lovelace firmly. "Is that all clear to you, Chief?"

Stukey hesitated, but only for a fraction of a second. Mr. Lovelace might be a fathead but you didn't say no to him in Pacific City when he asked for a yes.

"I got it," he said. "Me and Clint understand each other real well."

Mr. Lovelace stood up. He shook my hand again, then sauntered toward the door with his arm around my shoulder.

"I—uh—" He paused. "I—it has occurred to me that we have been rather inconsiderate here tonight. You have lost your—she was your wife, after all—and under such tragic circumstances. Yet we have allowed you to—we have called upon you to—"

73

"I am a *Courier* man," I said simply. "I have tried to act as I know you would have acted."

"I—uh—ahem—I am afraid you do me too much credit. In your case, I...Are you feeling entirely well? I was thinking that—uh—well, shock, you know. I would be happy to refer you to my own physician if—"

"Thank you, sir," I said, "but I believe the worst is now over. Now it is largely a matter of prayer, of consulting the spirit, of rising above personal tragedy into a newer and finer life."

"Well—uh—"

"Onward and upward," I said. "That is the answer, sir. My head in the clouds, my feet firmly on the ground."

I helped him into the car and closed the door. Dave took me by the arm, drew me away a few feet. "I'm sorry as hell, Brownie. I know how much—how you felt about her."

"A woman that wasn't my wife?" I said. "A youthful mistake? A floozy? A—"

"Brownie!"

"Yes, Colonel?"

"Is there anything at all—? Would you like to have me come back and stay tonight?"

"Why don't you?" I said. "We can talk over old times, our joyous carefree days in the army when—"

He let go my arm. He almost threw it away from him. Then he got a grip on himself and made one more try. "You did a swell job on Stukey, fellow. What you're doing—Ellen would have been proud of you."

"I wonder," I said. "I'll have to ask her the next time I see her."

"We'll get the guy who did it, Brownie! By God, we'll pour the coal on Stuke until—"

"Yes," I said, "we'll get him. Someone will get him."

"Well. . . . Think you'll make it all right? You wouldn't like to have me send out a doctor?"

"Send out a surgeon," I said. "I am heavily burdened and wouldst shed my balls."

He whirled and walked away.

I went back into the house. Lem Stukey had moved over to the lounge and was taking a drink from the bottle.

"Well, keed." He didn't seem particularly discomfited now. If anything, he appeared pleased, and I was confident I knew why. "It looks like we got to find ourselves a murderer, don't it?"

"Not necessarily," I said. "We, or rather you, have to look for one. You have to round up our local riffraff and eliminate them as suspects, also eliminating them from Pacific City."

"For nothin', huh? I drive all the easy dough out of town and I don't get nothin' out of it. That ain't reasonable, Brownie. I'm willing to play along with you—hell, don't I always go along with a pal? But you got to—"

"I don't got to," I said. "I've played along with you too long, Lem. Now I'm through."

"But why? You're sore about tonight? Jesus, pal, you can't blame me for—"

"I don't blame you. I'm not sore," I said. "Not in the way you mean. Something very bad has happened; that bad has to be offset. That's as close as I can come to explaining what I mean."

"And where do I come in? What do I get out of it?"

"Nothing more than you deserve. To put it succinctly, you do not get a murderer who is not one. You do not get some half-witted odd-job man and sap him into making a confession. It wouldn't work, Stuke, even if I were willing to let you do it. We

know the murderer is someone of fairly high intelligence. You'd
be laughed out of town if you tried to pin the job on one of your
typical fall guys."

"Yeah?" His eyes glinted. "So suppose I hang it on some
smart baby. Someone like you."

"You do that," I said, "and we'll discuss the matter again."

He stood up, slamming on his hat. He walked toward me
slowly and I crossed my legs, bringing one foot up in line with
his crotch. I hoped he would try something, but I was sure that
he wouldn't.

He didn't.

"Look, Brownie. Don't you see what you're doin' to me, pal?
It ain't just a matter of gettin' no credit—of knockin' myself
out and losin' out on all the easy dough and not getting no
credit for solving the murder. That's bad enough, but it ain't just
that."

"No," I said, "it isn't just that."

"You see it, huh? If I don't get the murderer—"

"If you don't get the murderer, or, let us say, until you do get
the murderer, you have to keep on looking for him. You won't be
able to let things get back in the shape they've been in. Yes, I see
that, Lem, and now that you see it I think you'd better leave."

He left, cursing. I waited until I heard him drive away, and
then I got up and stood in the doorway a few minutes.

It had stopped raining about an hour before, and now the
moon had come out and a few stars, and the air was clean and
balmy. I stood drinking it in in long deep breaths. I turned
and craned my neck, looking in at the kitchen clock. It was
only one, a few minutes after one. It seemed like years had
passed since—

And it was only a little after one.

I closed and locked the door. I went into the bedroom and turned on the light. I came back and turned off the living-room light. I started back into the bedroom. I went a few steps and then I dropped down on the lounge and began to cry.

About nothing, really; I suppose you would call it nothing. Certainly not over a problem. How can one cry over a problem? Or an answer — if there was an answer? I cried because — Just because, as kids cry, as she had used to cry. . . .

Because things were a certain way, and that's the way they were.

8

After a while I got up and went into the kitchen. I cracked four eggs into a glass, filled the glass with whisky, and tossed them down. I stood very still for a moment, swallowing fast, letting them get anchored. When I was sure they were going to stick, I took another drink and lighted a cigarette.

Another long time had passed, at least ten years. But the clock said twenty minutes of two. I refilled my glass with whisky and began cleaning the kitchen.

There was not a great deal to be done since the soot is more or less ineradicable and my meals at home are confined largely to eggs, milk, and coffee. But I did what little there was to do: scrubbing the sink, wiping off the drainboard and stove, sweeping the floor, and so on. I put the egg shells into the garbage pail and carried it out to the incinerator. I lingered a minute or two after dumping it, looking down at the railroad tracks. I often stand there at night, on the bluff overlooking the tracks, watching the trains go by, wondering if it wouldn't be better to...

But the last train for the night had passed more than two hours ago. The last one was the "milk" train—a combination freight and passenger that left Pacific City at eleven-thirty and loafed into Los Angeles some seven hours later. There wouldn't be another train until six forty-five.

I went back into the house and returned the garbage pail to its container. I filled my glass again and went to work on the living-room.

I cleaned it up — two-fifteen.

I cleaned up the bedroom — two thirty-five.

I made a stab at cleaning the bathroom (that part of the house that I have made into a bathroom) — two forty-three.

I had put a big pan of water on the kitchen stove and lighted a couple of burners under it. When it had heated, I carried it into the bathroom, climbed upon the ancient cast-iron stool, and, reaching upward and outward, dumped it into a five-gallon can that rested on a shelf near the ceiling.

I undressed and stepped under the can. I pulled a rope and the water rained down from a nozzle in the bottom of the can.

I put some clothes back on and mopped up the bathroom.

I finished at seven minutes after three. And I had never been more wide awake in my life.

Obviously it was time for stern measures. I took them — two full glasses, one behind the other.

I went to sleep then. Or, I should say, I lost consciousness. I didn't come out of it until a little after seven when the phone started ringing.

I sat up and looked at it. I mumbled what the hell and cut it out, for God's sake, and it went right on ringing. I rubbed my eyes and reached for the whisky. The bottle was empty, so I went out into the kitchen and opened another one. I came back into the living-room and sat down on the floor in front of the phone.

I slugged down a few drinks, lighted a cigarette, and eased the receiver off the hook.

I shouted "HELLO" at the top of my lungs.

I heard a clatter at the other end of the line, then someone breathing heavily. The someone was Dave Randall.

"Brownie . . . hello, hello, Brownie!"

"Don't yell so loud," I said. "It hurts my ears, Colonel."

"I hated like hell to bother you, Clint, but—can you come down for a while?"

"Come down? You mean to work?"

"Don't do it if you don't feel up to it, but I'm short-handed as hell. I've got three people working out of the police station— our friend Stukey is really bearing down on this clean-up campaign—and what with Tom Judge off sick I—"

"*He's* sick," I said. "I hope it's something serious?"

"It will be," Dave promised, "when I get hold of him. His wife called in to the switchboard this morning before I got down. I've been trying to call him back, but I haven't been able to raise anyone at their place. . . . How about it, Brownie? If you could just lend a hand for a couple of hours, just until some of the people in society and sports show up. . . ."

I let him wait while I took a drink. Then I said, "Well, I'll tell you, Colonel. I am a true-blue *Courier* man; I flinch from neither rain nor sleet nor Chamber of Commerce luncheons, but—"

"Never mind. Sorry to have bothered you," he said. "Take it easy and—Oh, yes, Brownie? Are you still there?"

"Yours to command, Colonel. Up to a point."

"I thought you'd want to know. They've got a red-hot clue to the murderer."

"So soon?" I said. "I think I'd better have a little talk with Mr. Stukey."

"He isn't pulling anything this time, Clint. It's the real thing. You know how those Golden Eagle cottages sit up on posts? Don't have any real foundation under them?"

"Y—No. I've never been around the island much."

"Well, some guy was crawling around under them last night. The cops figure that he may have been hurt when he—when he was struggling with her and crawled under there to pull himself together. Or perhaps he was just too scared or drunk to know what he was doing. Anyway, it looks like he must have been there not too long after the murder."

"Why does it look like that?"

"Why? Well, because of the imprint of his body, his hands and knees. They picked up several almost perfect handprints."

"How do they know they were made last night?"

"Because there wouldn't be any imprints, otherwise. Last night was the first time it's rained in weeks. There's a little seepage under the cottages and—Look, Brownie, I can't talk any longer now. I'll call you back the first chance I get."

"Don't bother," I said. "On second thought, I think I'll come down."

I hung up the phone. I sat there cross-legged on the floor, staring blankly into the black perforations of the mouthpiece as I reached for the bottle.

I tried to remember and, as I had last night, I drew a blank. I was bending over her. Then I was at the boat. And in between there was nothing.

My clothes...? No, all that water would have washed them clean in seconds. I couldn't remember, and there was no way I could find out. The finding out would have to be done by someone else.

Thinking, or rather, trying to think, I put coffee on the stove and went into the bathroom to shave.

I didn't believe I had crawled around under there. Surely, or so it seemed to me, I would not have wiped away my fingerprints only to leave a much broader clue. Then there was the matter of time. I had no recollection of events between my setting the fire and my arrival at the boat, but I did have a very strong impression that they were but briefly separated.

I hadn't done it. I was sure—almost—that I hadn't. It had been someone else. *But why would anyone else?* Probably some drunk had wandered out of a bar, or been tossed out, and he had holed up under the cottages for a snooze. He'd awakened when the cops arrived; he'd heard the ruckus and decided it would be a damned good idea to take a powder. And—

That was what had happened. I hoped.

I got cleaned up, and went into the kitchen. I poured whisky into an outsize cup and filled it with coffee.

I leaned against the sink, sipping it, taking an occasional long look at my hands. What I don't know about criminology would fill a five-hundred-foot bookshelf, but I'd learned at least one thing in my police-beat years: leaving or picking up a recognizable set of fingerprints is not as simple or easy as it is reputed to be. I talked to a detective one time who, on one of his off days, dusted and picked up prints throughout his five-room house. He didn't get one of himself or his wife or their two kids that would have served to identify them. This under so-called favorable conditions.

In mud, now, in anything as coarse as earth... Well, there

might be handprints, but fingerprints—huh-uh. I didn't think so. . . . I hoped not.

If Stukey had picked up a decent set of prints, even one good fingerprint, I'd have heard about it. By now, he'd have been printing me. Unless, of course, he was afraid of what I would do if he was wrong and he intended to do it casually. That would be Stukey's way, no doubt. To build the thing up big, and himself with it, then, say, to invite me to have a drink from a nice clean glass.

It was strange the way I felt. I hadn't given a damn for years, not a good goddamn whether I lived or not. And last night I had sort of tried to get the whole meaningless mess over with. I had taken a hands-off attitude in a gone-to-hell situation, and I had gone to hell and come right out again. And now I cared. Now I wanted to live. I wanted to badly enough to be afraid.

I turned the matter over in my mind, examining my emotions, probing their perverse strangeness, and, need it be said, consulting frequently with the whisky bottle. And so, gradually, I became clear-eyed and keen, and I could see my feelings for what they were—not abnormal but normal. Normal to a degree which, where I was concerned, would never do.

But there was no cause for alarm. I had known such feelings in the past, and down through the years their duration had become increasingly brief. They were in the wrong soil. They bloomed and withered almost simultaneously. I cared, yes, but only about a game, only about a problem, not about living or dying. It was an interesting game—the one interest without which there would be emptiness. And I wanted to win; I wanted to make *them* lose. But it was nothing to become fear-sick about.

Let them worry. With me it was only a game.

The old two-way pull began to assert itself. I headed for town, sitting very straight and circumspectly in the car seat but moving sidewise, mentally. Moving off to one side, off into a world known only to me, where I could see *them* without being seen.

Just a game. That was all I could win or lose. That was all *I* could do.

I parked the car in front of the Press Club and went upstairs. Jake, the officer of the day, was at his post. We went through maneuvers. We held close-order drill ending with a barrage. I stood back from the bar and we saluted.

"All secured, officer?"

"All secured, sir!"

"An excellent patrol," I said. "Everything is shipshape, jim-dandy, and crackerjack, and I hereby decorate you with the highest order of the land, the most coveted of awards, the—"

"On the house," he said, and he shoved my money back. "Look, Mr. Brown, maybe it ain't none of my business but shouldn't you be—"

I brought him to attention with a crisp command. I marched out and proceeded to the *Courier*.

Dave Randall hadn't exaggerated his need for help. He had taken a typewriter over to the city desk and was trying to do rewrite and his own job. The only regular rewrite man he had was Pop Landis. And Pop, nice guy that he was, was slow as all hell, and he was more than swamped with the running story of the murder and the crime clean-up.

I took his carbons off the hook and sat down at my desk. I began to read, briefing myself to take over, stopping now and then to write some minor but "must" story.

They had handled Ellen as delicately as they could without

distorting the facts. Our relationship was barely mentioned. The dirt would fly in the out-of-town papers, but here the emphasis was all on the murderer and the consequent criminal roundup.

I skimmed through the dupes... *long-estranged wife of Courier reporter, Clinton Brown... burial to be in Los Angeles... death attributed to asphyxiation...*

Asphyxiation? I read back through that part again, somehow glad that it had been that way.

...painfully but by no means critically burned, according to the coroner's office. The relatively minor nature of the burns, coupled with the fact that the mattress was almost completely consumed, indicates that Mrs. Brown must have revived soon after the maniac's departure. Panic-stricken and dazed, she was unable to find her way out of the smoke-filled cottage before succumbing to...

It was surmised that the murderer (for reasons best known to himself) had crawled about beneath the cottages. There were handprints, kneeprints, elbowprints (no mention of fingerprints). There was the imprint of his body, where he had apparently lain prone...

I paused. My heart did a small flip-flop — strictly, of course, because of the excitement of the game. I looked down at the typewritten page again. I read... and sighed with relief. *About five feet seven inches tall and rather heavy-set... shoes, approximately size eight....*

It wasn't me, then. Not by more than five inches and two and a half sizes. There was no way it could be twisted into being me. And whoever it was — some stumblebum, doubtless — he was safe; he wouldn't suffer for what I had done. Stukey would never find him. He didn't know enough about the guy, and what he did know fitted too many people.

I'd been working less than an hour when Mr. Lovelace came in. He gave me a startled look, then passed on by. He said something indistinguishable but obviously sharp to Dave Randall, and Dave followed him into his office.

He came out after about five minutes and scuttled over to my desk. Redfaced, almost cringing, he told me to beat it. "Right now, Brownie. The old man gnawed me out to a fare-thee-well. I knew it was a hell of a bad thing to have you come in to work right after—to handle a story about it. But I didn't know who the hell else to—"

"I would have been grieved," I said, "if you had not called me. I am wed to my work and stand ready at all times to do my husbandly duty, and I shall so inform—"

"Don't! For God's sake, Clint, just get out of here. If you want to do something, go out and see if you can get hold of Tom Judge. Tell him I said by God to get in here, and do it fast."

"Suppose he is locked in nuptial bliss with his wife? Do I have the colonel's permission to—"

"Brownie! Please!"

I stood up and slid my coat off the back of my chair, put it on, and picked up my hat. I—

I don't know what prompted me to say it; perhaps something in Pop's stories jogged my memory. Or, perhaps, it was the constant jangling of the telephones. I don't know why, but I said, "By the way, Colonel, did you talk to—did Ellen call in here yesterday?"

"Not that I know of. Why?"

"No reason." I shrugged. "She usually did call as soon as she hit town."

"Well, she didn't call yesterday to my knowledge. No one said anything about it. Why don't you ask Bessie?"

"I'll do that," I said, but I didn't do it.

I left the city room, walking right on past the cubicle where Bessie and her switchboard sat. I didn't want Bessie's memory jogged. I wanted her to forget that Ellen had called and that the call had been answered.

It was evidence, you see. Or, rather, it would be evidence if the person who had talked to Ellen could not satisfactorily explain his whereabouts on the night before. And little as I liked Tom Judge . . .

9

Lem Stukey's office was so crowded that I could hardly get in the door. He had two secretaries answering telephones; he was surrounded by reporters, our boys and those who had flown in from out of town; a dozen-odd cops and detectives milled around his desk. Being Lem, of course, with an eye ever to the main angle, he spotted me at once. And he pushed his way through the crowd and grabbed me by the hand.

"Jesus, keed, I'm glad to see you. Been thinkin' about giving you a ring, but... Let's get out of here, huh?"

He propelled me across the hall into an unoccupied jury room. He closed the door and leaned against it, mopping his brow with exaggerated dismay. "You ever see anything like that in there, pal? I ask you now, ain't that something?"

"Let me ask you," I said.

"You mean you ain't heard the news yet? I figured the boys at the *Courier* would be keepin' you—"

"I've heard, but it doesn't look like something yet. It looks like the old giant economy-size frammis. The old hoop-tee-do with a full year's supply of hot air. Any minute now you'll be announcing that you expect to make an arrest within twenty-four hours."

"Uh-uh. It's going to take me a little longer than that."

"Why should it? I can spot you fifty medium-sized, heavy-set guys of no specific age or coloring in five minutes."

"Pally"—he gave me a placating tap on the arm—"you sit right down there, huh? That's the keed. Now, you're still sore, ain't you? I jumped you last night. I tried to push you around, and—"

"And you got pushed around," I said. "And I'm not sore."

"I'm apologizin', Brownie. Let a guy apologize, won't you? I was all wrong, and whatever you handed me I had comin'. Jesus, I'd have been sore myself. A guy's wife gets killed, and the first he hears about it someone's tryin' to pin it on him."

"All right." I sighed. "I was sore. You've apologized. Now, all is forgiven and we love one another like brothers."

"You ain't just a-woofin', keed!" He nodded firmly. "Jesus, it almost makes me shiver when I think how I almost missed out on this. And I would have missed out on it if it hadn't been for you. If you hadn't've thrown the old hooks into me, I—"

"What have you got?" I said. "Just, by God, what have you got, anyway? Nothing. A bum crawls under those cottages to get out of the rain and—"

"Huh-uh. A bum with good shoes and a full suit of clothes? Huh-uh. Anyway, you don't find no bums over on the island. It takes a buck to get over and back on the ferry, and there ain't nothin' over there for them without dough."

"So it wasn't a bum, then. Just some guy who'd had too much to drink."

"That I'll buy. He—Now, wait a minute, keed." He held up a hand. "Let me give you the whole picture. You got a right to know and I'm goin' to give it to you. But under the hat, get me? I don't want to tip the guy off."

"You mean you picked up some fingerprints?"

"Fingerprints? What gave you that idea?"

"Nothing. Go on," I said.

"First of all—well, we done it last but I'll give it to you first—we raked the island from one end to the other. We went over that place with a—uh—"

"Fine-tooth comb?"

"Yeah, a fine-tooth comb, and we didn't turn the guy up, so we know he came over on this side. Okay. Now, get this. The ferry didn't begin running until ten-thirty last night; it didn't start back here with a load until ten-thirty. Then it didn't make another run until one in the morning, when it made its last trip of the day. Well, that last trip—"

"Let's skip the last one," I said. "The roundup was on by that time. The passengers were all checked and cleared before they were allowed to get on board."

"Right. Right on the nose. So that put our boy on the ten-thirty ferry. . . . Now, wait a minute, keed. I know what you're going to say: There was plenty of people waitin' to get back to this side, two hundred and four of 'em according to the ferry receipts, and you're going to say that stops us. But it don't, Brownie. It don't make it nearly as tough as it sounds. First you rule the women out. Then you rule out the couples. That cuts the total down to maybe sixty or seventy, just the stags."

"Which is still," I said, "no small number of people."

"Did I say no? But it don't look so tough no more, does it? Let me give you the rest of it. . . . We checked the hotels. The guy didn't show at any of 'em. We checked on the buses and trains. He didn't leave town. We checked the bay-side parking lots. He didn't pick up a car—"

"He could still have had one. He could have parked on the street."

"Not near the ferry, not unless he wanted to walk three blocks. And a guy on a party wouldn't do that to save four bits. . . . That leaves us the streetcars and taxicabs. The streetcars — well, that's kind of a toughie. We got to work from the fare zones, maybe check out whole neighborhoods. I say we got to, but I don't think we actually will. The guy's soaking wet. Everyone on the ferry was. He wouldn't want to screw around with no streetcars. I figure—"

"What about walking?"

"Well" — Stukey frowned grudgingly — "maybe. But it ain't very likely. It was pouring down rain. He'd be afraid of being picked up. . . . No, I think the taxis is where we'll get him. O' course, he probably didn't get out right at his house. And maybe he didn't go home right away. But—"

"In other words," I said, "if you check everyone in Pacific City, you may find him."

"Now, it ain't that bad," he protested. "It's going to take some time, sure, but we can do it."

"And after you do, then what? What have you got?"

"I got a killer. I got a guy that's got some goddamned tall explaining to do if he ain't a killer."

"And you'll have some to do. You're asking for it, Stukey. You're setting yourself up for the town's number one horse's ass."

He looked at me, puzzled. Still looking at me, he took out a cigar and lighted it, took a slow, thoughtful puff.

"I guess I don't dig you, keed. We been knockin' ourselves out on this. I thought you'd be tickled pink."

"Well" — I forced a laugh — "I appreciate it, of course, but if it doesn't lead to anything... You said yourself the guy was probably some drunk."

"He probably had a load on. It's pretty hard to hang around the island without taking on a load. But bein' drunk don't make him innocent; it's a hell of a lot more likely to make it the other way. A crazy killing like this, it's just the kind of a thing—"

"But there's so damned many loose ends, Stuke. The poem and—well—"

"So what? We just forget him because we can't dope it all out?"

"No, of course not. But—"

"Yeah?" His head was cocked to one side; his voice was a little too smooth. "Is that what you're sayin', pal? You want us to lay off the only hot lead we got?"

I laughed again, making it sound fretful and tired and jibing. "I guess I'm just not my usual cheery self today, Stuke. I'm not thinking like a *Courier* man. My ass is dragging, and the compass is pointing south."

"Well, sure. I can understand that. But—"

"Frankly," I said, "I think that seeing you engaged in honest work has thrown me into a state of shock. You have stunned me, Stuke. Such industry, such brilliance in one whose chief activity heretofore has been—"

He grinned, chuckled, and the puzzled look went out of his eyes. "That's the old keed. That's the old Brownie boy....All foolin' aside, though, pal, I'm doin' all right, huh? You got any suggestions, you just say so."

"I wouldn't think of giving you any," I said. "You're doing too well by yourself." I meant every word of it. I didn't have the slightest doubt that he would catch the guy.

He hooked his thumbs in his vest, trying to suppress a smirk of pleasure. "I got a hunch on this one, keed. I'd lay a case against a cork that he's our killer."

"Maybe. You may be right. But I imagine you'll have a hard time proving it."

"Huh-uh. A guy like that wouldn't be a pro. He wouldn't make you prove it. All we got to do is grab him and sweat him, and he'll cave in like a whore's mattress."

"That sweating," I said. "I would be very, very careful about that, Stuke."

"Am I crazy?" He leaned forward earnestly. "I got a plateful of gravy, and I spit in it? Not me, pal. Strictly legit, that's me. You put me on the right track, and I'm ridin' it clean to the end of the line. Incidentally, Brownie—"

"Yes?"

"I'll see that you get the story first. You personally. I'll keep the guy under wraps until—"

"You don't need to do that," I said.

"Don't need to? Hell, ain't we pals? Didn't you—" He broke off abruptly, blinking at me. Then his lips stretched in a slow, surprised grin. "Well, say, now! I—"

"That's right. If you get this man and if he is the killer, you can write your own ticket, right on up to and including county judge. I couldn't stand in your way if I wanted to."

He was in a generous mood. Moreover, I suspect, he was not at all sure that I wouldn't be of use to him. So he declared that purely out of friendship he would still see that I got first crack at the story. "Just because I love you, keed. But don't let out nothin' I told you this morning. If the killer got wind of it, it might blow the whole deal."

"I won't tell a soul," I promised. "In fact, it has suddenly dawned on me that I don't know any souls."

He snickered and said that was the keed, the old Brownie boy.

"Do you know any souls, Stuke? They don't have to be anything fancy. Just a good old-fashioned soul who would like to go steady with a badly frazzled id."

"The keed," he said, a trifle impatiently. "The ol' Brownie boy. Be seein' you, pal."

I left the police station and bought a fifth of whisky. Then I headed my car toward Tom Judge's house.

He lived in the corner house of a block-long double row of identical structures, all four rooms, all painted brown, all tar-paper-roofed with a little tin chimney near the back and another up front. Back when I was a youngster, and not a very young youngster, we called these affairs shotgun houses, and they rented for about twelve dollars a month. Tom's rent was ninety-five, which was just a little less than half his take-home pay.

The phone was ringing as I stepped upon the porch, and dimly, apparently in the rear of the house, a baby was crying. I knocked and the crying stopped abruptly. Then, after a moment or two, the ringing stopped also.

I knocked again, long and loudly. I tried to open the screen. It was locked. The shades at the window and door were drawn. I leaned back against the porch rail, opened the bottle, and slugged down a stiff one.

It was the first drink I'd had since my morning patrol and it refreshed me wonderfully. I bought two more and then, of course, accepted one on the house. I left the porch, walked around to the rear, and pounded on the back door.

The baby cried again. For a split second. Otherwise silence.

I took a drink. I drew back my foot and kicked the door as hard as I could. It flew open and I walked in.

10

Mrs. Judge was standing in a corner near the stove, holding the baby to her breast. She wasn't twenty-five, I knew, but she looked ten years older. Flat-chested, unhealthily fat through the hips, thin-necked. You don't live very high on the hog when you're married to a semi-incompetent reporter on a small-city newspaper. You age fast.

Her face was made up, her hair was in curlers, and both jobs had obviously been done in a hurry. She looked at me trembling, wide-eyed. I gave her a reassuring smile and looked at Tom.

An open trunk stood on the kitchen floor. He had been packing it, and he was still holding an armful of clothing. Slowly he let it drop, and his mouth opened and closed silently.

"Going somewhere?" I asked.

"N-No. N-No, Brownie." He gulped and shook his head. "J-Just s-storing a f-few—"

He wanted to act sore; he knew he should. But he just wasn't up to it. He looked haunted, as gray-pale as a sheet of copy paper.

"I—I—" He gulped again. "I heard about your wife, Brownie. M-Midge and I h-heard it over the radio, and I'm s-sure s-sor—"

"Easy," I said. "Just take it real easy. You've not been particularly fond of me. The feeling has been reciprocated. But this is a friendly visit. Now, how about a drink?"

"I—I d-don't—"

I uncapped the bottle and pushed it at him. "Take it," I said. "Take a big one."

"You take it, Tom." Mrs. Judge spoke for the first time, giving me a half-defiant look. "Tom doesn't drink much. He's not used to drinking. He—he-he—"

"I know," I said. "Your drink, Tom."

He almost snatched the bottle from my hands. He tilted it thirstily, gagged and shivered, and thrust it back at me. A little—a very little—of his usual belligerent assertiveness returned.

"Well, Brownie"—he hiccuped—"I know you're probably upset about your wife, but that's no reason to—"

"Friendly," I said. "I said it, and I meant it. I'm here to ask you some questions and give you some answers."

"Yeah? You are, huh? What makes you think—?"

"Maybe you don't want to. But I think you'd better listen before you make up your mind."

He hesitated, looked at his wife. Her eyes moved to my face and her lips began to tremble. "He's good," she said. "Y-You— he's told me about you! He t-tries so hard, h-he works twice as hard as you do, a-and—all you can do is make fun of him! H-He—I—it's your fault! Y-You can p-play around and everything is s-so easy for you, and h-he—"

"No," I said. "No, it isn't easy for me, Mrs. Judge."

"It is! He told me how it is! You make fun of him because it's easy for you and—and you can blow in all your money on yourself, and all he can do is—is—" Her voice broke and she began to sob.

Tom said, "Midge, honey. You shouldn't—"

I said, "It's all right. I understand how Mrs. Judge feels; I think I understand how you've felt. But I'm trying to be your friend now."

She brushed her nose against her arm and gave the baby a little pat. She looked from me to him and nodded. "You talk to him, Tom. You take another drink."

Then she shuffled out of the room and elbowed the door shut behind her. I sat down at the table and he sank down across from me. I had a drink. I waited until he had taken one.

"All right," I said. "Here's the first question. My wife called the office yesterday afternoon. You talked to her. What was the substance of your conversation?"

"W-What—what makes you think—?"

"She always called as soon as she got in town. She didn't talk to anyone else or they'd have told me about it. Your desk is right across from mine. You'd have answered my phone."

"B-But—but I'm not always there!"

"She'd have kept ringing until she got an answer. And if she hadn't got one she'd have called the city desk."

He stared down at the cracked oilcloth of the table, his fingers fumbling at the pocket of his shirt. I took out my cigarettes, put one in his mouth, and held a match for him.

"I'm not sore, Tom," I said. "If I were sore I wouldn't be sitting here. And you wouldn't be either—very long."

"W-What?" His head snapped up. "What do you mean?"

"You know what I mean. But let's take it from the beginning. You talked to her. You got her to give you the number of her cottage. Then you told her I was gone for the day, and you suggested something to the effect that you would be happy to take my place."

His dull, chubby face reddened and he spread his hands. "Brownie, I — I — Christ, what can I say?"

"It's all right. You behaved quite normally. You haven't had much of what passes for good times. No later than yesterday morning I'd called you a lousy newspaperman and a son-of-a-bitch. Why not put one over on me through the pleasant medium of laying my wife?"

He shook his head miserably. "Brownie, it — that's not quite —"

"It's close enough. What did she say to the proposition?"

"Well...she didn't really say anything. She just sort of laughed."

"And you construed that as an invitation? Go on."

"Go — go on?"

"Spill it. Tell me all. Go and on. A phrase meaning to proceed."

I felt sorry for him, responsible for him. But he didn't need to make it twice as tough as it was by acting like a Piltdown moron.

"You went over to the island," I said. "Take it from there and keep going."

"I...well, I went over around four. A little after four, I guess it was. A little while before the storm started. It was still light then, of course, and I didn't want to — to go down there yet, so I stopped in a bar. I had a couple of drinks and —"

"Did you see anyone you knew?"

"Huh-uh. I mean, I don't think there was anyone there that knew me. I didn't talk to anyone or...Well, it started raining, pouring down, but drinks were awfully high in there and someone said the ferry had stopped running and I didn't know quite what to do. I'd been kind of nerving myself up. I'd got to thinking about how crazy this was—me with a wife and kid, and you, a guy I worked with—how it might get me in all kinds of trouble. And—and I'd just about decided to drop it. I mean it, Brownie! If the ferry had been running or if I'd had enough dough to hang around there in the bar, I—Jesus, Jesus! Why couldn't it have been that way? Why—"

"I wonder," I said. "Go on, Tom."

"There wasn't anything else to do, so I did it. I bought a fifth at the bar—tequila, the cheapest thing they had. Then I went down to her cottage. I figured we'd—we, we'd just drink and talk and as soon as the storm was over...All right, all right"— he paused and sighed—"go ahead and laugh."

"That was a grimace," I said, "of unadulterated pain."

"Yeah? Well, anyway, I guess you know what happened. She wouldn't let me in. She bawled hell out of me, said I'd taken a hell of a lot for granted, and slammed the door in my face. I— God, Brownie, it wasn't right! If she hadn't wanted me to come, she ought to have said so. She shouldn't have laughed and acted like, well, it would be all right."

"Very few of us," I said, "behave as well as we should. Perhaps you've noticed that...I take it that, having no other refuge, you retired beneath the cottages?"

"Yeah, hell. What a mess. Soaking wet and damned near broke, and I had to lay under there like a goddamned rat or something. Couldn't even sit up straight, and it wasn't a hell of a lot dryer under there than it was outside. I kept crawling around, trying to find a dry spot. I guess most of those places were empty but there was one—well, you could hear the bed going up and down, and then the people getting up and going to the bath-room and—and—and me under there like a rat. Like a god-damned drowned rat. You—I guess it wouldn't have meant anything to you, Brownie. But—hell, what difference does it make? I opened up the tequila and started hitting it. I kept pouring it down, I was so damned miserable and wet and...All at once I went out like a light. It was just like something had hit me over the head.

"I don't know how long I was out. I came to all of a sudden and I couldn't figure out where I was. I was scared as hell, and I heard someone pounding and a bunch of guys calling back and forth. And I could see flashlights shooting around on the ground. I remembered where I was then and that really chilled me. All I could think of was that the place was being raided and what the hell I was going to say if they found me. I crawled up to the end where the street was, and then I ran across into that little park and—I don't know where all I did go. It was still so damned dark and raining so hard. I think I passed out a couple of times. Then—I don't know how long it was, but finally I heard the ferry whistle and I cut down to the landing. There was a big crowd there, and they were all wet, too—I mean they'd got pretty wet in the rain and most of 'em were stiff or half stiff from hanging around the bars all evening. I squeezed onto the ferry with 'em and went straight down to the john. I was down there in one of the stalls, having a few drinks when—"

"You'd kept the tequila with you then? That's good."

"Yeah, I'd held on to it somehow. So I thought I'd got out of the mess without any real trouble, and I was trying to pull myself together when these two guys came in. Boat hands, they were. They were talking about a woman being killed over in the cottages, and—and I didn't think about it being her b-but, God, I'd been there and I'd been crawling all around and—and—and then I got home and Midge and I turned on the radio, and—"

"How did you get home?"

"I took a taxi—all but the last five blocks. I only had sixty cents, see, so I rode out fifty cents' worth and gave the driver a dime tip and walked the rest of the way."

"You didn't give him your address?"

"No. I just had him head up Main and down Laurel until the meter showed four bits, and then I got out."

That was good in a way and bad in a way. The driver didn't know where he'd gone, but he'd remember him. And a neighborhood like this, particularly a neighborhood like this, would receive a thorough going-over by Stukey's boys.

"Y-You—" Two big tears were in the corners of his eyes. "I've t-told you the God's truth, Brownie. I d-don't need to—You know I didn't kill her, don't you?"

"Yes, Tom," I said. "I know you didn't kill her."

"B-But they think I did! They've got evidence! They know I was there. They know what I look like. They—"

"They don't," I said. "Get me? They don't. They know a guy of about your build and size was there, but that's all they know."

"That's all they need! That cab driver and knowing what I look like and—! I've got to get away, Brownie! It's the only thing I can do!"

"It's the one thing you can't do," I said. "They'll be watching the trains and buses. If you did manage to get out of town, they'd trail you down. You'd be hanging a sign on yourself."

"B-But—"

"The cab driver will be mistaken, if and when they turn you up. It'll be your word against his. Yours and . . . What about your wife? She knows about this? She'd swear that you were at home all evening?"

"Sh-She —" His voice dropped to a whisper. "She knows. Sh-She'd swear to it. But —"

"Good. That'll be good enough. You both stick to that story and there's not a damned thing they can do. They'll try to, of course, if they find you. . . ." If, hell! They'd find him, all right, but I didn't want him any more frightened than he was. "Just deny everything and keep denying, and they'll have to let you go."

He lifted the bottle, slowly set it down untasted.

"I — I d-don't think I can do it, Brownie. They get to questioning me and —"

"You've got to. Once they place you on that island at the time of the murder, once they get you to admit you saw her, that she refused to let you in and you laid around under those cottages drinking —"

"I know. Jesus!" He shivered. "It's all I've been thinking about. They'll think I was sore at her. They'll think I hung around to — to —"

"Right. So you do what I told you to do. Don't admit a damned thing."

"B-But — but they'll get me all tangled up! I . . . I don't think I can take it!"

"How about the gas chamber? Can you take that?"

He buried his face in his arms and began to sob. I watched him for a minute and then I reached across the table, grabbed him by the hair, and jerked his head up.

"Now, listen to me," I said. "You didn't kill her and you're not going to let anyone talk you into thinking you did. You're absolutely safe. A rough seventy-two hours is the worst they can give you. That's all, and then it's over. You can take it. I know you can. *Know* it, Tom; get me? If I didn't think so, I wouldn't say it!"

He tried to work up a smile, not much of one, but it was a large improvement on blubbering. "Y-You're swell, Brownie. You really think I can—?"

"Didn't I say so? Now, get yourself shaved and whatever else you have to do, and come on with me. I'll drop you off at the office."

"Office? Oh, God, no, Brownie. Not to—"

"Yes, to the office. They need you. It looks bad to lay off." I stood up and pulled him up. "Get moving. You can tell the colonel your phone's been out of order if he gives you any guff. He'll probably be so glad to have some help he won't say anything."

It was like pulling teeth to get him started, and even after we were in the car and on our way downtown he kept on arguing and pleading, begging to be let off. He "just couldn't do it" and "everyone would know" and "I'm s-sick, Brownie" and so on, until I almost decided to take him home and let come what might. Not because I was irritated by him—although I was—but because I was afraid my efforts were being wasted. For if he had no more stamina than this, if he behaved this way now, he wouldn't hold out five minutes against Stukey. He'd cave in right away, and since that was the case...

But perhaps he would stiffen up; perhaps, given a day or so, he would become his usual resentful self, a man dedicated to the proposition that what was demanded of him should automatically be withheld. Perhaps the very arrogance and in-turned sullenness that had got him into this mess would get him out of it. It seemed logical that it would. Fate would have to be very cruel indeed to reform his dully dogged spirit now.

So I resisted his begging. I gave him drink for his stomach and steady pep talk for his nerves, and if the bottle was exhausted — and it was — by the time we arrived at the *Courier* building, it had nothing at all on me.

Sighing heavily, Tom opened the door and slowly eased one foot out to the curb. He hesitated, then suddenly turned around again.

"Brownie. I —"

"No," I said. "No, no, no, no! Think of the brave little woman. Think of the wee kiddie. And drag yourself to hell upstairs!"

"I'm going, Brownie. But I may not see you again and you've been so swell —"

I groaned. I removed my hat and slapped myself on the forehead.

He frowned slightly, but he didn't budge. "It's about Dave. He's always been nice enough to me and you — well, you know how you've been. But things are different now. Maybe Dave's never done anything against me, but you've done plenty for me. We're on the same side, and anyone that's got it in for you —"

"Got it in for me?" I said. "Not that there is anything serious in my sniping at the colonel — the colonel understands my playful nature — but aren't you just a little confused?"

"I know." He nodded. "You're all the time riding him, and maybe you've been asking for it. But that doesn't cut any ice with me. You start noticing him, Brownie. Notice how he'll load you up—try to swamp you with work—when he's got other guys doing nothing. And he's always getting you out of the office, shooting you out on assignments. He doesn't want you around where you can shine up to the old man. He's jealous and—"

I stopped him. Strangely, or perhaps not so strangely, I was angered by what he said.

Dave was my own particular little target, and I wasn't going to have anyone else tossing darts at him. They had no reason to; there was such a thing as being fair. If Dave kept me loaded with work, it was because of the high percentage of incompetent staffers such as Tom Judge. If he tried to keep me out of Mr. Lovelace's way, it was because of a well-warranted fear that I might do or say something irreparably embarrassing.

I said as much, in a properly oblique way.

"I want to set you straight on this, Tom," I said firmly. "Dave would be the last person in the world to do anything to harm me. He's so constructed that he'd feel strongly responsible for any misfortune I suffered. I know; he's proved it. Every time I've lost a job he's quit also and hired me on at his next paper."

"Maybe he was afraid not to. You might have hung around drinking and needling him, giving him so much trouble he'd get fired himself."

I wouldn't have done that. Dave wouldn't have had to put up with it if I had done it. All he would have had to do was reveal a certain secret, and I would never have shown my face in another newspaper office.... Of course, if he did reveal it—

It was as though Tom were reading my mind, reading a thought that had never been there until now.

"It's none of my business, Brownie—but you got something on him? I mean, did he pull a bad boner somewhere or—"

I shook my head, to myself as well as him. A boner, yes, but there'd been hundreds and thousands of boners, and the war was a long time over. It was simply a mistake. No culpability had attached to it then, and certainly none could now.

Dave had nothing to fear from me. He put up with me only because of his own stricken conscience. Naturally, he didn't want—

"Dave's all on edge, Brownie. It wouldn't take much to throw him completely. He's got a lot of dough tied up in a house here, and he's not a kid any more, and newspapers are folding all over the country. If he thought he might lose out here—"

"He won't. There's no reason why he should," I said. "You're utterly and completely wrong, Tom. Dave and I are actually pretty good friends. If we weren't, he'd have fired me long ago."

"No, he wouldn't. The old man wouldn't let him. Why, I'll bet if you took a notion to knock him to Lovelace he'd—"

"Go on," I said. "Just get the hell up there and get to work. You're the boy with the troubles, remember? Well, don't forget it. Just forget about me, and remember what you have to do."

He nodded grudgingly, climbed out, then leaned back inside again.

"You watch him," he said. "Sneak a look at him sometime when he thinks your back is turned. You'll see. That guy could kill you and enjoy doing it."

II

I held midday maneuvers at the Press Club; early in the afternoon I stopped by the coroner's office. He was a stuffy, conceited bastard. He wasn't at all sure when he could release Ellen's body, but he "thought" he might be able to do it by Friday.

I pointed out that this posed a difficult situation. It would mean that the burial couldn't take place before Sunday, which might be impractical for the undertaker and undoubtedly would increase his charges. Moreover, it would crowd me seriously for time, if I was to be back at work on Monday morning.

He shrugged. My troubles, he indicated, were no concern of his.

I have never got along with coroners. They are either laymen of the lower orders who must pretend to be much, or they are fatheaded medical failures who are sore at the whole world for that which only they have wrought.

Our discussion continued on an increasingly less amiable plane. I finally suggested that if he simply had to have a body around I would buy him one from the local rendering plant, a cow, horse, or anything he named, and when he tired of playing with it he could stuff it—he, personally, and not a taxidermist.

That did it. Ellen's body would be released Saturday, he said, and not a goddamned day before. Meanwhile, I was to get out of his office and stay out.

I got out and called Dave. As I saw it, the funeral couldn't be held before late Monday, or more than likely, Tuesday; in other words I would probably be off until the following Wednesday.

Dave hesitated, studying the calendar, I imagine. He said it would be all right, he guessed. He'd have to get Lovelace's okay, but he was sure it would be all right.

"How about coming out to the house for dinner before you leave?" he added. "Do you good to get some home-cooked food. Kay told me to ask you."

"Good, sweet Kay," I said. "Dear, kind Kay. Tell me, Colonel, wouldn't you say she has a truly wonderful soul?"

"Good-by," he said shortly. "I'll talk to you when you're not half stiff."

"You misunderstood me," I said. "I said *soul,* not—"

"Look, Brownie," he snapped. "I'm trying as hard as I know how to—"

"You're fed up with me, aren't you?" I said. "You've had it up to here. It would suit you fine if I dropped dead."

It slipped out involuntarily.

Dave made a sound that was midway between a grunt and a gasp. I didn't blame him for being startled. I was myself.

He was silent for a long moment; then his voice came back over the wire, worried, warm with concern. "Look, boy. Where are you calling from? I'll come and get you and take you home."

"I'm sorry, Colonel," I said. "Sergeant Brown presents his apologies. I have become patrol happy; the maneuvers have got me clobbered."

"They must have when you talk like that. Where are you calling from?"

"I'm all right," I said. "Forget it, forgive it, and God bless you. 'Twas a slip of the tongue and nothing more."

"But...I just don't understand. Of course, I get a little annoyed with you at times, but I thought you knew how I felt about you. Entirely aside from friendship, you're the best man I've got. I couldn't run the place without you."

"Thanks," I said. "Thanks a lot, Dave. I said a damned foolish thing, and I'm sorry, and let's leave it at that."

"Well...look." He was still troubled. "I was thinking about that dinner invitation. Naturally, you don't feel up to social occasions so soon after—afterward. Why don't we make it next week, sometime after you get back from Los Angeles?"

I didn't want to make it any time. My idea of an agonizingly misspent evening was one in the company of Kay Randall. I was afraid to refuse, now, however, in view of what I had said to Dave. He would think I had meant it. And somehow— whatever I felt about him and however I acted—I did not want him to think that.

So I accepted with thanks, and a mental note to kick Tom Judge's tail. I went home, knocked myself out with booze, and fell asleep.

The next day, Thursday, I had another talk with Lem Stukey. He hadn't turned up anything with the streetcar company, and he'd had the same result with the taxi operators. But he was by no means discouraged.

"We didn't expect nothing on the streetcars." He shrugged. "Just checked them out as a matter of form. The bastard took a cab, and don't think hell ain't going to pop when I turn it up."

"But you've already—"

"We've checked the trip sheets, we've talked to all the drivers who worked that night. Now we pull 'em in one at a time and find out which one's lyin'. Don't you worry none, keed. He's makin' it tough for us—and he'll sure as hell regret it—but he ain't making it impossible."

"I don't get you," I said. "Why would he lie about it?"

"Probably got a criminal record. Afraid of getting mixed up with cops. Or maybe his license has run out. Hell, there's all kinds of reasons. Maybe he knocked the fare down. Maybe he did a hit-and-run and doctored his trip sheet to put him in another neighborhood."

"You amaze me, Stuke," I said. "I had thought you cunning but never intelligent." And I realized, with further amazement, that Stukey was constantly coming up with little things like that, things that maybe didn't stamp him a genius but that sure as hell proved he was no slob.

"We'll get him," he promised. "We're just gettin' warmed up."

I left Lem and paid a visit to the express company and an undertaker. I made a long-distance call to a Los Angeles undertaker and repaired to the Press Club. Dave had been trying to reach me. I called him, immediately following maneuvers.

He had talked to Lovelace, and it was all right for me to lay off the extra time. Perfectly all right. However—

"Oh-oh," I said. "Pray proceed, Colonel, while I hoist my pack and rifle."

"I wouldn't ask you myself, Clint. The old man wants you to handle it if you possibly can. It's a pretty big thing, and..."

He gave me the essential details. The president of one of the Mexican Federal banks, immediately across the border, had embezzled several million pesos. The fraud hadn't been made public yet, and the president, who was en route from New York after a vacation, was unaware of its discovery. But he was due to be arrested as soon as he stepped off the plane in the morning. I was to be on hand to get the story.

I should point out here, perhaps, that the yarn wouldn't have been a big one in New York or Chicago. For that matter it wouldn't have got a very big play in Los Angeles. But because of our geographical location — because it concerned a neighboring city, although a Mexican one — it would be of prime interest to our readers.

I agreed to handle it.

I got up at six in the morning. At seven I was at the border city's airport, where I met the plane.

The president was on it, but so also were two Federalistas. They had got on at Los Angeles, and they took charge of Señor Presidente as soon as the plane touched in Mexico. They hustled him into a waiting limousine and sped away. I learned that they intended taking him fifty miles down the coast to another city, but that was all I learned.

I called Dave. He talked with Lovelace while I waited. The decision was for me to continue to the second city.

I did. The president had been put aboard a government plane and was on his way to Mexico City.

So there went my story, for the local authorities could give me no information on the case. The chief of police, a surprisingly young, friendly guy, sympathized volubly and insisted on drinking his lunch with me.

We drank and drank *and* drank, tequila mainly with an occasional mescal and chasers of that wonderful creamy *cerveza*—beer such as I have seldom tasted outside of Mexico. The chief became very gay. It was too bad, he said, that I was driving a car. Otherwise he would take his car and we would go to the island together—"your Rose Island, Cleent"—and then I could cross over to Pacific City on the ferry.

I blinked, rather owlishly, according to the mirror in the back bar. I said, "Now, wait a minute, *amigo caro*. Just how in the—?"

"You do not know, yes? You think I keed, no?" He grinned delightedly. "Come. I show you."

He led me over to the wall, stabbed a shaky finger at a framed map of Baja California. The finger weaved, slid, and came to a stop at a point near the Mexico-California border.

"Here is—*hic*—is how you say, pen—pen-in—?"

"Peninsula."

"Yes. Pen-in—well, you see eet, yes? How way out here eet come? Yes. And here is teep of island. And here...what you say is here, Cleent?"

"Something never to be taken internally," I said. "An insipid beverage, somewhat salty in this instance—"

"Ha, ha. Is water, you say, yes? You be wrong, Cleent. *Poquita, sí*. Two, three inches, yes, but no more. Underneath is beeg—how you say?—reef. Rock. Like pavement."

"You're joking," I said. "You mean to tell me you can drive a car from here to here?"

"*Sí.* Many time I have. Many peoples they do. Like I say, is rock. *Muy bueno camino*—ver' fine road."

Many peoples they do, but I never had. In fact, I had never heard of the reef. It wasn't so surprising, I guess; I seldom got over to the island. I could do all the drinking I wanted to at home or in the Pacific City bars. And as far as the cat-houses went—

So you see, I had no reason to know much about the island, and how you got there other than by ferry or charter boat.

But still, the information disturbed me. It was an extra little item in a story I thought I knew pretty well letter-perfect. Now I saw I didn't know it all. It was another piece of jigsaw puzzle that I thought I had all locked together.

The information shouldn't *really* have disturbed me. Since Stukey knew everything else that might possibly be of use to him, he doubtless knew of this land route to the island. And he had quite properly ignored it as a factor in shaking my alibi. I couldn't have made this roundabout round trip on the night of the murder; I wouldn't have had time. For that matter no one could have done it during the storm. To have driven across almost four miles of reef—almost three times the width of the bay—to have done that on a pitch-black rainy night with a heavy sea running, well, it was simply out of the question. It was many times as fantastically dangerous and impossible as what I had done.

It had no bearing, then; otherwise, Stukey would have mentioned it and have looked into it. It didn't affect me. It didn't affect Tom Judge. It didn't—it was meaningless. But somehow it bothered me.

It lingered in my mind, nagging me, long after I had shaken hands with the Mexican police chief and headed back toward the border. I reached the U.S. customs station early in the afternoon. I knew several of the guards there, and I asked them about the reef. They knew about it, of course. It wasn't worthwhile to keep a customs officer there, but it was kept under observation by the border patrol.

I wondered about that—whether any very close watch had been kept on the night of the storm. I doubted it like hell.

We talked a minute or two more, and I mentioned casually that they had probably had an easy time of it during the storm. They admitted as much. "Sat around on our cans all evening, Brownie. Didn't a thing cross over but one taxi."

"Do you re—?"

I cut off the question abruptly. I didn't want them curious, and anyway, they couldn't have told me anything. A dark stormy night outside and a snug, comfortable guardhouse. And cabs always got a very fast check. They weren't searched as private passenger cars were. There would have been a quick glance through the window, and fast, "Birthplace? U.S. citizen?" and then a wave onward—dismissal.

I drove on, still vaguely disquieted. I stopped in Pacific City for a few groceries and some bottles and went on out to the house. I mixed eggs and whisky. I drank them, took a bottle into the living-room, and sat down on the lounge. I got up and sat down on the floor. I stared at the telephone.

Tom Judge was on a very bad spot. Stukey was certain to find him soon unless he was diverted from him. An element of doubt should be introduced; another person should be brought into the case. Why not push that reef business at Lem? Talk it up to him? Why not sic him on that lone taxicab that had crossed the border? Point out that a man might have gone down in a cab, and *walked* across on the reef?

No, no. No! That was stupid. Lem would already have thought about it. Crossing on foot would have been even more hazardous than by car. And what would have been the purpose in it, anyway? What could he—Dave Randall—have hoped to accomplish by it? To catch me there, perhaps? To go in after I had left and—and—?

And nothing. It was reasonless. It was impossible. Absolutely without basis. How in the hell had I started thinking about this? Why did I persist in so thinking?

A taxicab had crossed the border. There was a submerged reef connecting with the mainland. And that fathead Tom Judge had said Dave had it in for me.... That was all I had to go on. The reef, the cab, and the twisted imaginings of Tom, a guy who was always trying to stir things up, dividing the world into enemy and friendly camps, and attaching to first one side, then the other. And out of that—and despite the fact that I *knew* who had killed Ellen—

But did I know? She'd got up after I left. Somebody had wiped away fingerprints. She'd died of asphyxiation, not—

Suddenly I laughed out loud. I laughed so hard that the whisky slopped out of my glass. For at last I'd remembered, and I was almost foolish with relief.

Dave had been at home that night. Stukey had called him there and then Dave had called me. Everything had been happening at once, and I guess I'd been halfway off my rocker, but now I remembered. Dave had been at home. The colonel had been in the bosom of his family, tossing the wee ones on his knee perhaps while the little woman hummed a happy roundelay....

I sat drinking and thinking, musing idly, trying to sort out my feelings about Dave. They were pretty confused.

In a way, I liked him; I felt sorry for him. Yet there was another side of me that hated him, that was determined to make him go on suffering for what he had done to me. I wanted him to steer clear of trouble for two reasons. Because I liked him— because I hated him. He was a nice guy—and I wanted him to stay right where he was. Where I could get at him, dig at him day after day until...

I don't know. It is hard to be specific about one's emotions. It is difficult to stop a story at a certain point and give a clear-cut analysis of your feelings, explain just why they are such and such and why they are not something else. Personally I am a strong believer in the exposition technique as opposed to the declarative. It is not particularly useful, of course, when employed on an of-the-moment basis, but given enough time it invariably works. Study a man's actions, at length, and his motivations become clear.

12

I drove up to Los Angeles on Sunday and took a room at the Press Club. The Pacific City undertaker got the lead out of his can and the one in L.A. did likewise, and the funeral was held late Monday.

It was a nice funeral, I thought. Stukey and the Randalls sent flowers, also Mr. Lovelace and the *Courier* staff. Too, the newspaper lads I knew in Los Angeles had bought a couple of big bouquets, and there was one giant-sized wreath without a card on it. I didn't think much about it. I supposed that it had been bought by the city hall crowd in Pacific City and that the card had been lost.

There were four press cars in the funeral procession. They were there on business, the boys were, since the story was still news. They had to shoot pictures and get me to do some surmising about the killer and so on, enough to pad out into a few paragraphs. But I was acquainted with most of them, and having them there was good. It made the thing seem more like a real funeral.

They were on overtime at the end of the ceremony. So the reporters phoned in their stories and the photogs sent in their plates by motorcycle courier, and we all went to the Press Club.

We bumped a couple of tables together and started drinking. We had dinner and continued drinking.

Luckily, they wouldn't let me pay for anything. I had to borrow on my car to bury Ellen, and I was very, very short of money.

A waiter came up with a telephone call slip. I looked at it, casually, and shoved it into my pocket. I didn't recognize the number. I couldn't recall knowing anyone by the name of D. Chase. It was probably some friend of Ellen's, I thought. Someone who wished to offer condolences.

The party broke up about nine, and I bought a bottle and went up to my room. As a tried and true *Courier* man—one who did not need to be watched to do his duty—I suppose I should have driven back to Pacific City that night and gone to work Tuesday morning. But I was tired, and there was much heavy thinking to be done. And something told me it could not be done amid the hustle and bustle of Pacific City's greatest and only daily.

I stood at the window of my room, gazing out and downward. A fog had settled over the city, and the lights bloomed up out of it, blurred and hazy. Now and then there was the muted scream of a siren as an ambulance weaved northward through the traffic to Georgia Street Receiving.

Los Angeles. Sprawling, noisy, ugly, dirty—and completely wonderful. It would always be home to me, this place and no other. It would never be home to me.

I turned out the lights and dragged a chair up to the window. I cocked my feet up on the radiator and leaned back.

Tom Judge: at the outside, Stukey would have him in a day or two. Logically, he should have run him down before this. And exactly what was I going to do about it?

Tom might be able to hold out. He might be able to take a seventy-two-hour sweat—the three-day "investigation" period in which his sole hope and defense would rest on his own personal guts.

As I say, he might. But there was at least a fifty-fifty chance that he wouldn't. And once he broke down, it would be too late for me to do anything.

If only the murderer could have been tied in more closely with the poem. That is, if it could be established that the poet and the murderer were the same man. So far the poem had drawn very little attention. It had been mentioned by the police, paraphrased in various papers, and that was all. Ellen had had it, for reasons known only to herself. Dazed and dying she had grabbed it up—doubtless accidentally. That was the official attitude, and it was too bad that it was that.

Anyone who knew Tom would know him incapable of the poem. A few paragraphs of plodding prose were Tom's literary limit.

So it was unfortunate that the poem had been brushed off so lightly. It was unfortunate that there was not some way of proving that the murderer and the poet were one and the same man.

The phone rang. Softly, in actuality, yet it seemed loud and ominous, as phones do at night in dark hotel rooms.

I frowned at it. Then, I stretched an arm out and lifted it from the writing-desk. A husky, feminine voice said, "Mr. Brown—Brownie?"

"Who is this?" I said.

"I'll bet you can't guess. I'll bet you've forgotten me already."

I sighed. I said nothing. There is nothing much to say to

people who ask you to guess their names while betting that you have forgotten them.

"It's Deborah, Brownie." She laughed a little uncomfortably. "You know, Deborah Chasen."

I remembered. I said something then, but I don't recall what. Something like: "Well, how are you?" or "What are you doing here?"

"I'm fine," she said. "I've been here all the time, Brownie. I was—I heard about your wife."

"I see," I said.

"Yes," she said. "I heard about it, so I didn't go. I've been waiting here for you. Did you get the flowers I sent?"

"Flowers? Oh, the wreath," I said. "I wondered who it was from."

"I sent them for you," she said. "Just on your account, Brownie, not hers. I'm not sorry about her. I'm glad."

"Well, that's very nice of you, Deborah," I said. "I see you're still your subtle, tactful self. Now, if you'll give me that horse laugh of yours my evening will be complete, and I'll go to bed."

She did laugh; then her voice went soft and throaty. It was as though she were breathing the words rather than speaking them.

"Brownie, darling—isn't it wonderful? I was just sick when I left Pacific City that afternoon. I wanted to die; I would have, too; I didn't care about anything any more. And then the next morning I read that—about her! It was like being born again, Brownie. Honestly, I was just so happy I cr—"

"Jesus, God," I said. "What kind of a woman are you? Do you realize that you're talking about my—"

"I don't care. You love me; I know you do. We love each

121

other, and she was in the way. Now—well, now she isn't....I want to see you, darling. Shall I come over there, or do you want to come over here to my hotel?"

I cursed her silently. It was on the tip of my tongue to say that I was leaving immediately for Pacific City, but I caught myself in time. As surely as hell was full of sulphur, she'd follow me there.

"Deborah," I said, wearily, "you are a goddamned pest. I don't want any part of you, or any other woman. I've tried the double harness once and I damned well got a belly full of it, and I'm playing it alone from now on. I—"

"Pooh. I'll change your mind."

"Nothing will change my mind," I said. "Now, I suggest you take a nice cold shower and eat a couple of pounds of saltpeter and—"

"Oh, Brownie!" She laughed delightedly. "You sweet crazy thing you! I'll come over there, darling."

"No!" I said. "No, wait a minute, Deborah. I do want to see you, naturally, but I've had a pretty rugged week and I...Well, why don't we let it ride until tomorrow, baby? I'll give you a ring, and perhaps we can have lunch and a few drinks."

Silence. Then the sound—sounds—of a cigarette lighter clicking, and a long, slow exhalation. I could imagine the green eyes narrowing, hardening.

"Brownie," she said, quietly.

"Try to understand, Deborah. Put yourself in my place. My wife was killed less than a week ago. I buried her today. Now you expect me to—"

"Brownie."

"Well?" I said.

"I was doing all right before I met you. I didn't have anything, but I didn't expect anything. Then y-you—you know what you did, Brownie. You didn't tell me you were married. You held me and kissed me, and y-you...you did a lot of things I wouldn't have let you do if I'd known. And then you—now you—"

"Deborah," I said. "Just put it this way. Just say that I was a heel and I still am, and let it go at that."

"No! You're not, Brownie. You couldn't be if you tried.... Boy!" She sniffed. "I'm an expert on heels! I know all about 'em, and I know...So what is it, darling? Is it the money? Are you afraid I'll embarrass you? Are—"

"Wait," I said. "Wait a minute, Deborah."

"I'll do anything you say, Brownie, Anything! Just d-don't— don't drive me away from you."

"Wait," I repeated. "I've got to think."

She waited. I thought. And, of course, I didn't need to, I already knew what I would have to tell her, prove to her if necessary. That I simply couldn't provide what she above all women would want.

She would be sorry, doubtless, perhaps even angry, but there would be no further argument; she would have no illusions about its importance. Deborah might have a very beautiful soul, but it was no good at all in bed. She would be stunned at the idea of substituting a fireside chat for a good hard roll in the hay.

So...I would have to tell her. But I couldn't do it over the phone. I couldn't—I didn't think I could make it stick—and I didn't want to.

I wanted to see her one more time.

"There's a little bar near here," I said. "A couple of blocks south on Main. It's called the Gladioli. If—"

"I'll find it. I'll be there. Right away, Brownie?"

"Right away," I said.

I put on a clean shirt and a fresh tie. I combed my hair in front of the dresser mirror, and suddenly I drew my arm back and hurled the comb against the glass.

My reflection tossed it back at me. His lips moved, and he cursed, and he asked why the hell it had to be this way. Why, if he didn't have the other, did he have to have all this? He said oh, you're a pretty bastard, you are. A knock-'em-dead son-of-a-bitch. They turn around to look at you, they stretch their goddamned sweet necks to get a peek. And...and that's all there is. Only what they can see. I don't get it, by God! Why, when there's nothing to do with, do you have to look like...?

The reflection shrugged. He said, that's the way it was, so that's the way it was.

Then he reached for his coat and turned wearily away. And I turned off the light, and left.

She was there ahead of me, standing up near the glazed front of the place, peering anxiously up and down the street. I came up while she was looking the other way, and she whirled around, startled, taking a swift step forward so that for a moment we were pressed against each other. I gave her a little hug, and she said, "Brownie! Oh, *Brownie!*" and gave me a harder one.

We entered the dimly lit bar. She let go of my arm and led the way to a rear booth, rounded hips swinging, slim-ankled, full-calved legs stretching and pressing impatiently against her skirt, horsetail of corn-colored hair brushing the small, square shoulders. She had a mink stole draped over her arm. She was wearing a thin white blouse and a tailored fawn-colored suit.

They made her look bigger in all the big places and smaller in all the small ones.

We sat down on the same bench of the leather-upholstered booth; she pulled me down beside her. A sleepy-looking waiter brought drinks and went away again.

"Brownie," she whispered. "Brownie, darling...." And her breast shivered against my arm.

She pulled my face down to hers and we kissed. And then gently she pushed me away again.

"I'm terribly sorry, Brownie. I must have sounded awful. It was just that I love you so much, and I know how mean she must have been and—"

"She wasn't," I said. "Foolish perhaps, but not mean."

"Well, anyway, I'm sorry. I'm—you won't have to be ashamed of me, Brownie. You just tell me how you want me to be, and whenever I get—"

"Deborah," I said, "listen to me."

"Yes, darling."

"I'm—there's something I have to tell you. I should have told you in the beginning, but it's not an easy thing to talk about and—well, I didn't think it was necessary. You were leaving. I never expected to see you again."

"Yes?" She lighted a cigarette. "What is it, Brownie?"

"I can't marry you. I can't sleep with you."

"Oh?"

"No! That was the trouble between me and my wife, why we were separated. I couldn't be a husband to her."

"Oh...I see. And all the time I thought—" The green eyes flashed happily and her face broke into a smile. "That doesn't mean a thing, darling! Not a thing."

"It—it doesn't *mean* anything?" I said.

"Why, of course, it doesn't! It was the same way with me and my husband. You just...a certain person simply isn't the right one, and you get to where you not only can't—"

"Listen," I said. "You just don't understand, Deborah. What I'm—"

"I know. I know exactly what you mean. I—No, let me tell you, Brownie. You've got a right to know, anyway. Even after he died, I couldn't. I tried—I'm human and I—I—well, I tried; just like you have, probably. And I couldn't do it. It was like there just wasn't any such thing as far as I was concerned. I'd lost all desire for it, and I was sure it was gone for good. I was sure until that day in Pacific City when I—"

"Deborah," I said. "You don't know what you're talking about. What I'm talking about."

"You think I don't." She laughed. "You just think I don't, Brownie! That's why I was so completely broken up when I found out you were married. I knew it had to be you or no one; that if it weren't you then there simply wouldn't be anyone....You'll see, darling." Her voice sank to a throaty, caressing whisper and her eyes burned like green fires. "It'll be all right for both of us. It'll be like nothing ever was before...."

You see, you do see, don't you, how very hard it was? How even I, with stalwart purpose in my heart and lofty motives in my mind, might hesitate? She had to be told, yes, and certainly I intended to tell her. But she was making it so hard and she was so sure of herself, so positive that everything was now all right, so happy....And in a way I loved her.

Her small hard hand moved under the table and came to rest on my thigh. It moved down, up, down, up. It stayed up, pressed there firm yet trembling. She shivered and leaned against me.

Then, that sleepy-soft whisper again: "You've made me so happy, darling, and I'll make you so happy. You'll see, Brownie. You'll never be sad again."

"Sad?" I said, and I pressed the buzzer for the waiter. I needed one more drink. I would tell her after the second drink. "You are speaking in paradoxes, Deborah. I am a jolly *Courier* man, a member of the happy *Courier* family. We know no sadness, only joy in a job well done."

"You're sad," she said. "That's why you write those terribly sad poems."

13

The waiter came and went, came back with drinks and went away again. In the interim, while we were waiting for him to get out of the way, we made meaningless small talk.

He left for the second time. She sipped her drink, her fingers toying with the cardboard menu, a faintly teasing smile on her lips.

"Surprised you, didn't I? You thought it was a secret."

"A very rare type of secret," I said. "One dealing with the non-existent. Newspapermen don't write poetry, Deborah, never, never, ever. That's traditional."

"Oh, ye-es?" she drawled, smiling. "I know one that does. He was writing one the first time I saw him. In the office. He got rid of it very fast, but not quite fast enough. . . . Not for someone who could read a menu upside down and across the table."

I lifted my glass. I took a very long swallow and set it down again. "Poetry," I said. "It places me in a pretty bad company, doesn't it? I mean, that poem she had. They think there's a possibility that the killer may have written it."

"Do they?" She shrugged. "Oh, well. . . ." Just, oh, well. Meaning nothing; meaning a great deal.

"Yes," I said. "That's what they think, and I have a strong

hunch they may be right. I think they may have even more reason to think so in the not-too-distant future."

Here was my answer. Just a matter of minutes before—in
my hotel room—I had been wondering how I could draw
Stukey's attention away from Tom Judge, how I could prove
once and for all that the murderer and the poet were the same
person.

Now I knew how I could prove it.

Through Deborah.

If, say, there was another murder, and if a poem similar to the
first one was found on the victim...

"Let's not talk about...it." She frowned. "But you won't
write any more of those poems, will you? I think they're bad
for you."

"I think they could be, myself," I said. "I certainly wouldn't
care to have them become a matter of public knowledge,
Deborah."

"Don't you worry, darling." She patted my thigh. "I'd never
tell anyone. Now you just stop being sad, hmmmm? Because
there's nothing to be sad about, now."

"Perhaps not," I said. "How can one be sad when he has the
sky and the stars to gaze upon and God's own green carpet to
rest his aching arches? Morning's at seven, Deborah. Morning's
at seven, the hillside's dew-pearled, God's in his heaven, all's
right with the world."

"That's awfully pretty, Brownie. Did you write that?"

"Yes," I said. "I did it under my pen name, Elizabeth
Khayyam. I wrote it one eventide on a windswept hill while
watching a father bird wing home to his wee ones. There was a
long caterpillar in his beak and he had it swung over his

shoulders, muffler fashion, as a shield against the wintry cold. I...Listen to me, Deborah! For God's sake, listen!"

She had been laughing, looking at me fondly. Now she went serious and she said, "No, Brownie. Whatever it is, I don't want to hear it. Not tonight, anyway."

"But you just don't—"

"You don't know everything about me either. What's the difference? I just don't care, Brownie! We're together and we're going to stay together, and that's all that matters. Oh, it's so wonderful, darling. Just think! Me, finding you, getting you back after I thought I'd lost you. The only man in the world I could—"

"Please," I said. "I—The world's a hell of a big place, and—please, please—"

"No. No," she said. "I won't listen. I only know I'd die without you. I don't want to hear anything that might—I don't want to hear anything. I don't need to. It wouldn't matter. Nothing about her or you and her or....It wouldn't matter, Brownie. I—I—I wouldn't care if you'd killed her!"

She nodded firmly, her eyes somehow cold yet burning. Up near the bar, the jukebox suddenly began to blare, shaking the walls with its clamor before someone turned down the control.

I took a cigarette from my package. I lighted it and inhaled, slowly, stalling for time.

Had the poetry meant anything to her? Had she been hinting, giving me a warning, when she said that it was bad for me? Did she know that I *had* killed Ellen, and...?

Probably she wouldn't care now—that is, if she did know. She could rationalize that. Ellen was no good. Ellen would have had it coming to her. Ellen was nothing to her, and I was everything. *But—*

But what about later when she discovered that I was not everything, that I was nothing? That I was merely another blank page in her book of life. How would blunt, straight-to-the-mark Deborah Chasen behave then? She would have no use for me—would she? And I knew what her attitude was toward people for whom she had no use. "She was dead, and I was so happy...." Wasn't that what she had said?

Perhaps I could tell her the truth and it would be all right. But if it wasn't all right—if she turned spiteful and vengeful—I'd be sunk. It would be too late to draw back, too late to try to silence her. I'd have lost the game, and there wouldn't be another one.

So...?

I tamped out my cigarette and swallowed the rest of my drink. "Your fabulous fanny," I said. "Is it quite comfortable, Deborah? Then keep it where it is while I procure my car and carpetbag, and we shall then head south into the dawn."

She let out a delighted squeal.

"Brownie! You sweet, funny... But hadn't I better—?"

"We will send for it," I said. "Whatever you need we will send for, Deborah. Meanwhile, with me providing a toothbrush and you providing yourself we shall want for nothing. We shall have paradise now."

She smiled, looking a little puzzled through the tenderness, but she didn't argue. She was right up on top of the load after a hard climb, and she was going to do nothing to upset the applecart.

"Do you believe in a personal paradise?" I said. "A personal hell?" Do you have a soul, Deborah?

"Hurry," she said. "Hurry as fast as you can, darling. We get in your car, I'm going to take this girdle off."

I hurried, but I was quite a little while at that. Because I had something more to do than get my car and check out at the club.

There was a hotel up the block and on the opposite side of the street. I remembered its arrangements well from the days when I was working in Los Angeles and covered conventions there.

Immediately inside the lobby entrance, a staircase led to the mezzanine. A little beyond the head of the stairs was the public stenographer's desk. She wasn't there at this hour, naturally, but her typewriter, a silent machine, was, and her wastebasket hadn't been emptied.

I sat down, dipped into the basket, and selected a discarded second-sheet with only a few lines at the top. I creased it and tore them off.

I turned the paper into the typewriter.

The poem went very fast; I suspect that I was lifting it, at least in part, from my original manuscript. When I had finished, I laid it on the desk and scrubbed both sides of the page with my handkerchief. I folded it, using the handkerchief, picked it up with same, and stuffed it into my pocket. . . .

I am somewhat hazy in spots about the ride to Pacific City, but my general recollection is that she enjoyed it immensely. Not that I didn't—although my mind was not exactly pleasurebent—but I didn't matter. I meant it to be her party, and I believe it was a dilly.

The highway was practically barren of traffic. I had had the foresight to lay in a plentiful supply of beverages, and I saw to it that she sampled them generously. We rode southward into the fog, her laughter growing louder and louder. She braced her feet against the dashboard and raised her hips off the seat, trying to remove the girdle. She tried it a half dozen times, and each time she'd barely get started when laughter overpowered her. She flopped back in the seat, snickering and sputtering and guffawing. She hugged me around the hips, giggling and choking, shivering against me.

"B-Brownie, you — you s-st.... Ha, ha, ha, ha — y-you s-stop n-now, B-Brownie...!"

"You bray like a goddamned jackass, Deborah," I said. "Like a bitch baying at the moon."

"B-Brownie! Now, that's not in...ha, ha, ha, ha...."

"Shall I breed you, Deborah? Is your tail tingling, my prize bitch?"

"Ha, ha.... D-don't talk about d-dogs, Brownie. I — I — Oh, d-darling...ha, ha, ha, ha...."

She was so wonderfully earthy and human. Eve before the apple, Circe with the giggles, Pompadour on a night off.

About thirty miles out of Los Angeles, I turned the car onto the beach and got out. I opened the door on her side, and she lay back with her legs stuck out and her skirts up, and I got a good two-handed grip on the girdle.

I gave a hell of a yank.

Well, I got rid of the thing, the girdle, and I found out something. About her size. However big she looked in certain places, she wasn't actually; it was simply the way she was built. There just wasn't enough of her to be big. As a man with some experience in such things, I'd say that she couldn't have weighed much more than a hundred and ten pounds.

So I yanked, thinking there was much more ballast than

there was, and the girdle skidded off of her. My hands shot upward and backward, flinging the girdle into the ocean. I stumbled and fell flat on my back. Then she was out of the car and beside me.

She sat back, looking down at me almost gravely. And the sand felt peaceful and soft and warm, and so did she.

"You're very soft," I said. "Very soft and warm, Deborah."

"I don't have any pants on," she said. "I guess that's why I feel that way."

"I'll tell you something," I said. "You'll never die, Deborah. There is no death in you, only life. So long as there is laughter, so long as there is warmth and light, so long as there is soft flesh, fresh and sweet-smelling like no perfume ever made, so long as there is a breast to cup and a thigh to caress . . . you'll live, Deborah. You'll never die."

"That's awfully pretty," she said. "Want me to tell you something?"

"Please do," I said.

"I don't care if I do die. Not now, Brownie. Not after tonight."

We drove on to Pacific City.

We got to my shack just before dawn.

And I killed her.

14

I didn't kill her right away. As a matter of fact it was that night, more than sixteen hours later. Just as I was about to decide that I wasn't going to do it.

You see, the two-way pull wasn't working as it should. It was pulling on me, trying to jerk me out into that other world, but she was pulling, too, pulling me in the opposite direction. And she was stronger than it was.

It was strange, very, how strong she was, how one so small could be so strong. I didn't believe that I could kill her. I was afraid to do it. I wasn't afraid of being caught, you understand. I was quite sure that I wouldn't be, and, since I am writing this some weeks later, you are aware that I was not. It was a fear away from and beyond the purely personal. It was as though she were life itself, the root of all life, and when I killed it, that, her, all life would vanish.

And I had visions of a parched and withering earth, a vast and empty desert where a dead man walked through eternity.

I didn't think I could kill her.

It is hard to believe that I did.

Even now, now more than ever, as I sit here alone in the *Courier* city room, and I am above self-delusion and below

135

reproach — now when my one task is to set the record straight — it is hard to believe that I did it.

I find myself thinking that there must have been someone else, someone who knew about her and —

But, of course, I did do it. The act of murder is not to be forgotten quickly, and I remember the facts of this one well. I did it . . . but not then. More than two thirds of a day passed, in the meantime, and I think you should be told about that.

I think we should keep her alive as long as we can. . . .

I parked the car at the side of the house, and we went inside. She went to the bathroom while I drew the shades, and then she came out and I went.

She'd slept for about the last hour of the ride, and she was fairly wide awake now. She stood in the center of the living-room, smiling at me a little timidly as I came in, and she said she bet she looked a sight, didn't she?

"Awful," I agreed, and I gave her a kiss on the mouth and a small swat on the rear. "A hung-over hussy if I ever saw one. You must have a drink and pull yourself together."

"Oh — uh —" She hesitated. "Do you want a drink, Brownie?"

"It gags me to think of it," I said. "But I shall force it down. I will not let you drink alone."

I fixed us two whopping drinks and brought them into the lounge. She curled up at my side, pulling my arm around her, and we sat there drinking and talking. And saying very little. A train thundered by, leaving the house a-tremble. She pulled my arm tighter, pressing my hand against her breast.

"Brownie. You're . . . you're not still afraid? I mean, you don't think it might not be all right?"

"I am sure it will be," I said. "In such a package only quality could prevail."

"No, really, darling. If you're —"

"Really," I said. "Honest and truly. And you have your whole life to prove it to me."

"Mmmm," she said, and she wriggled. "Promise me something, Brownie? Don't die before I do, I wouldn't want to live without you, darling! Without your love."

"I promise," I said. And after a moment I added, "We will die together, Deborah. That is the way it will be. When you die, I will die."

"Will you, Brownie? Would you really want to?"

"I don't think," I said, "it will be a matter of wanting."

We drank. I kept filling our glasses. She asked me if my legs didn't get awfully stiff from driving, and wasn't I awfully tired. I said that they did indeed, and that I didn't get so much tired as tense. As soon as I got limbered up and relaxed a little . . .

"Brownie," she said.

"Yes?"

"I — nothing."

Several minutes passed; five or it might have been ten.

"Brownie —"

"Yes?"

"Nothing."

We went on drinking. I began to have a hard time keeping up with her. Finally she mumbled something about getting a sleeping pill, and she started to get up. Then she fell back, letting her head slide down into my lap.

She stared up at me squinting, drowsy and dizzy. One of her

fingers wobbled and wavered, pointing at me. "Y-You know what? Y-You j-jus' got one eye. P-Poor Brownie o'ny got one eye...."

"The other one is turned inward," I said. "It is examining my soul."

"Mmmm?" she mumbled. "Jus'—just got—"

Her eyelids closed, and her lips parted and stayed parted. She slept.

I carried her into the bedroom and put her on the bed. I loosened her brassiere, took off her shoes, and pulled the spread over her. Then I went back to the lounge.

I poured another drink, but I didn't take it. Exhaustion suddenly overpowered me, and in a split second I was sound asleep....

When I awakened, the phone was ringing and she was kneeling at the side of the lounge, shaking me.

I started to sit up. I flopped back down again, yawning and rubbing my eyes. I looked at her, dully, wondering who she was and how she had got here.

"The phone, darling," she said. "Hadn't you better answer it?"

"Phone?"

"It's been ringing a long time, Brownie. Shall I answer it for you?"

That brought me awake, or much more awake than I was. It brought back my memory. I asked her the time, and she said it was a quarter of three.

"Probably the paper." I sat up, yawning. "Let 'em ring. If they knew I was back, they'd wonder why I hadn't come in. Might want me for something even this late."

"All right, Brownie. Want to go back to sleep again?"

"Yes—no," I said. "How about some coffee?"

"I've got some made, darling. I'll get it right away."

She went out into the kitchen. The phone stopped ringing. I sat looking down at the floor, at the blanket which must have been covering me.

It didn't necessarily mean anything. Neither it nor the fact that my shoes were off and the buckle of my belt unfastened. When you have drunk as long and as much as I have, you do a great many things without remembering or thinking about them. Just automatically. Frequently I have undressed and put myself to bed without ever knowing that I had done it.

So this, the condition I had awakened in, was doubtless more of the same. But so long as she was awake, it seemed like a good idea for me to be. She might be getting curious. She might become actively curious if she had the opportunity. *Maybe she already had.*

I washed while the coffee was heating and held brief and silent confab with that strange guy in the mirror. He looked a little haggard this morning—I suspected an incipient case of cirrhosis of soul—but withal he seemed reasonably at peace. He was strongly of the opinion that Deborah should not be killed.

"Unnecessary, my dear man," he advised me. "I suspect, as you did originally, that she is not greatly endowed with sharpness. She is not stupid, of course; she can be not-sharp and not-stupid, also. She is just a very natural, very lovely, very simple and straightforward woman."

"Yeah, sure. But she said—"

"A manner of speaking; we all say things like that. But—assume that it was not. Let us say that she saw the connection between the poetry and Ellen's death. It didn't change her love for you. She went right on loving and trusting you. Would she, then, feeling about you as she does, suddenly turn on you because of something you cannot help? And — to make another far-fetched assumption — suppose she did? You have an airtight alibi, haven't you? You couldn't have crossed the bay that night. So, what if she should — ?"

"I don't know," I said. "I don't know to all the questions. The deal's so goddamned screwed up and — and I can't take chances — and there's Tom Judge. I don't know why the hell they haven't nabbed him already."

"What about Tom Judge, anyway? The fact that there's another murder and another poem while he's in custody won't necessarily establish his innocence of the first one."

"It will throw considerable doubt upon the matter of his guilt. I'll do the rest. After I talk with Mr. Lovelace, and Mr. Lovelace talks with Mr. Stukey, Mr. Judge will be released. And promptly."

"We-ell...I suppose so. But — want to make a small bet? I'll bet you don't kill her. You can't."

"You think not, huh?"

"I *know* not. You can't kill her, Brownie. If she gets killed, it won't be by you."

She'd whipped up some toast and scrambled eggs along with the coffee, and it tasted better than any food I'd eaten in a long time. She'd already had a bite, she said, but she had coffee with me. We sat at the table, smoking and drinking coffee, making quite a bit of conversation but saying very little. She hadn't slept a great deal, she said. She'd had a hard time sleeping in recent years and had come to depend heavily on sleeping pills. Having taken none before retiring, she'd been pretty wakeful despite the booze.

We moved into the lounge after a while, and she sat with her legs drawn up, her head resting against my shoulder.

"Brownie," she said. "Am I keeping you from anything? If there's anything at all you have to do—"

"I'm doing it," I said. "This is what most needs doing right now."

"I thought you might get me that toothbrush...if you're going out. I could use one."

"I may have to go out later on," I said. "I'll get whatever you need then."

It occurred to me suddenly that it might have been Stukey calling a while before. He might already have Tom Judge. But...no, it wasn't likely; it must have been the paper checking on me. Stukey wouldn't have stopped with a call. Knowing me as he did, he would have come out to see if I was there.

We drank, or rather, I did. Deborah barely sipped at her glass. The afternoon—what there was left of it—slipped away and darkness came. And she never asked that we—that we go—

Deborah stirred lazily. She stretched, arching her breasts, and stood up. She asked me if I wouldn't like her to fix something to eat, and I said, well, I would have to give the matter some thought. We were discussing it when the phone rang.

I glanced at the clock: seven straight up. There wouldn't have been anyone at the paper for hours.

I picked up the receiver. It was Stukey.

"We got him, keed. It'll knock you flat when you hear who it is."

He told me who it was. Tom Judge. It did not surprise me in the least.

"Good God!" I said, putting a good heavy exclamation mark behind the phrase. "It's incredible, I never liked the stupid jerk, but I wouldn't have thought — Has he confessed yet, Stuke?"

"There ain't hardly been time yet. We just pulled him in. But he's our boy, all right, pal. He fits all the specifications, and he's got that old guilty look written all over him."

"And he's been identified, of course? By the cab driver."

"We-ell, no." He hesitated. "The taxi angle didn't pan out. We picked him up on an anonymous tip. Came in on the switch-board, and that dumb ox we got workin' there didn't trace —"

"What about his wife?" I said. "She admits he wasn't at home that night?"

"We-ell" — again a pause — "no. But, o' course, she's lyin'. . . . He's it, Clint; I'd swear to it on a stack of Bibles. How soon'll you be down?"

It was my turn to hesitate, and I did, lengthily. Then I let him hear an uncomfortable laugh.

"This one kind of throws me, Stuke," I said. "If it was anyone else but him — another *Courier* employee. You see what I mean? There's no real evidence against him. Suppose you had to turn him loose, and I had to go on working with the guy?"

"Well, yeah. But, keed, I *know* this baby is —"

"You knew the same thing about me. Remember?"

"Naw! No, I didn't," he protested. "I couldn't find you any-where and I figured you was the only one with a motive, and — and I was sore. But I knew you hadn't done it as soon as I cooled off. I didn't have that ol' hunch like I got about this guy. Why, hell, Clint, I —"

"I'm not throwing it up to you," I said. "I'm just pointing up the possibility that you might be wrong about Judge. . . . I think I'd better steer clear of this for the moment, Stuke. Anyway — unless Judge cracks before then — I want to talk with Mr. Lovelace before I get personally involved."

"Well, yeah," he said grudgingly. "I see what you mean."

"He'd be damned sore, you know, if Judge wasn't guilty. He'll probably be damned sore, in any case. The idea of a *Courier* man being a murderer won't sit at all well with the old boy."

"No. . . ." There was a thoughtful silence. "I guess he won't like it much. But, looky, keed, I ain't playing hotsy-totsy with no murderer just because —"

"You're damned right you're not," I said. "If you did, you'd have me on your tail. All I'm saying is that I'd better keep out of the frammis until I talk to Lovelace, unless Judge spills in the meantime. You can hold him seventy-two hours, can't you?"

"Well, sure. But —"

"I'll let it ride, then," I said. "I'll talk to Lovelace in the morning and get in touch with you afterward. I'd do it tonight, but we can't break the story before morning, anyway, and Lovey gets pretty hot if he's bothered at night."

Stukey grunted, cursed under his breath. He said, "Well, I sure as hell hate to . . . What you think, keed? I ought to go pretty easy on this character until you get the word? Just kind of leave him alone and let him stew?"

"I wouldn't want to advise you," I said. "I don't have much use for Judge, and — well, you know, my own wife and all. I might give you the wrong dope."

"Uh-huh. Sure. Well" — he sighed — "you'll buzz me in the morning, then?"

"As soon as I talk to Lovelace."

We said good night and hung up. I was reasonably confident that he would give Tom little trouble tonight. And by morning...

By morning?

She knelt down in front of me, resting her elbows on my knees. "Brownie. Is it — is there something wrong?"

"They think they've got the man who killed Ellen," I said. "One of the boys from the paper. I — it's hard to believe that he's guilty."

"Poor Brownie. It's just one thing after another, isn't it? Want another drink, darling? Something to eat?"

"No," I said. "I don't think I do."

"Why don't you get out for a while, darling? Ride around and get a little fresh air. You must be getting awfully restless."

"Well, I —"

"You do that, Brownie." She cocked her head to one side, smiling at me. "Pretty please? I'll lie down while you're gone."

I grabbed her in my arms. I hugged her, burying my face in her hair. "God," I said. "Jesus, God, Deborah. If you only knew —"

"I do know," she said. "You love me. I love you. I know that, and — that's enough."

"I wish it was as simple as that," I said. "I wish —"

"It is, Brownie. It *is* that simple."

I kissed her.

I left the house and drove away.

I drove up on the hill first, up into the Italian section of town, where I had a few drinks at a bar. Then I bought a bottle in a liquor store, pulled the car onto a side street, and sat there drinking alone in the dark.

I drank for a while. I wondered...about her, about Ellen. About myself.

Why? I asked. Why had I done what I had to Ellen? That was a mere by-phrase with her—the "you burn me up." An imbecile would have known that, and I was not, by the most exaggerated estimate, an imbecile. I had had to kill her—*perhaps*—and perhaps I would have to kill Deborah. But the other...

Was it because...well, hadn't she always been hysterically afraid of fires? And Deborah—wasn't she morbidly afraid of dogs?

I tried to look at myself squarely, to think the thing through. I couldn't do it. Something kept getting in the way, bending my vision around into a circle; and while I was in that circle I was not of it. It did not touch me. Between the man who wanted to look and the man to be looked at was a heavy curtain. Drawn, of course, by the inner man.

It was now after nine o'clock. I gave up the searching and started home. I wasn't going to kill her; I knew that much, at least. There was no need to—no real reason—and I wasn't. And...

And suddenly there was a reason, many of them, and I was going to do it. The two-way pull had me to itself. All resistance had ended abruptly, and I was swung far out into that other world. There was nothing to hold me back. It was as though she had suddenly ceased to exist.

I let the car coast into the yard quietly, the motor stilled. I eased the door of the house open. Silently, I went in.

The kitchen had been cleaned up and the dishes put away. The living-room had been swept and put in order. I hesitated, looking around, and it was ridiculous to feel that way, in view of what I intended doing, but I was troubled, worried about her.

To have left her alone, in this isolated railroad-side shack....
She'd have been helpless, although she'd have doubtless tried to fight. And if there'd been a scuffle, the house might be like this. Put to rights, and...

I went into the bedroom.

I heaved a sigh of relief.

She was all ri—she was there. Stretched out on the bed on her stomach. She was lying with her face in the pillow, her arms akimbo on it, the horsetail of corn-colored hair hanging down to one side.

So quiet. So peaceful and calm and trusting. So...quiet.

Actually, she must have been one of those nervous sleepers. You could see how she had been balled up tight; you could see it by the way the sheets were wrinkled and the mattress depressed. Now, finally, she had straightened out, her body stretched out full length. But she was still tense, her fingers sticking out rigidly, her whole body stiff, unbending, motionless.

That's how she lay there, and I heaved a sigh of relief, and I killed her.

I stood over her, staring down, studying her position: the way her neck formed an unsupported bridge between the pillow and her shoulders.

I stooped down at her side, balling my hand into a fist. I raised it, brought it down hard.

There was a dull pop, and her neck sagged and her head bent backward.

I picked up her purse, put the poem in it, lifted her in my arms and carried her out to the car.

It was all right. It was a game again. I had been forced to play and with an inordinately heavy handicap. And I had won, and she perforce had lost. But...

But already I was feeling the emptiness, the lifelessness.

And off in the not-too-distant distance, it began to move toward me... *The withered and dying world, the vast and empty desert where a dead man walked through eternity.*

I reached the dog pound.

I threw her over the wall.

15

I...I am going to get through this part very quickly. About the next morning, that is, the discovery of the body—what was left of it—and...and so on. I got through it rather well at the time. I had the crutch of work—pressure—and Tom Judge's situation. And I had to do it. And it was a game. Now, however—

Now, I shall have to get it over with quickly.

I must do so....

The story broke about five minutes before deadline, and I handled it. It was short, thank God. The paper was already made up, and there was only one brief yarn that the news editor could yank. So this one had to be short also. There wasn't a whole lot to say, for that matter, since the body had only been discovered a few minutes before.

Those half-starved dogs were always fighting and raising hell, and the Peablossoms—the old couple—hadn't investigated the racket until morning. By that time, of course, there wasn't much left of... Well, they'd identified her by the contents of her purse: by, among other things, a nearly empty box of sleeping pills with her name on it.

I say *they'd* done it, meaning the cops, not the Peablossoms. They'd also found the poem in her purse.

There was no way of knowing how long she'd been dead, whether she'd been killed there and tossed into the stockade or whether she'd been brought there after being killed. The only clue to the murderer was the poem.

The Peablossoms hadn't heard a car during the night, but then, they wouldn't have heard one with the dogs carrying on. There were a great many footprints and tire tracks around the place. Far too many to be of value as clues.

Well, I wrote the story. Then Dave and I were called into Lovelace's office for a conference.

He was in a very bad humor, and he took it out on Dave. This "Judge fellow." He'd always known he was no good, should've been fired long before. Dave should've fired him. Now he was a murder suspect—a *Courier* man under arrest for murder! Shocking. Inexcusable.

And Deborah Chasen—*that* woman! She, it appeared, was also Dave's fault. An editor was supposed to know what was going on, wasn't he? He was supposed to have news sources, people who kept him informed? Well, why, then, hadn't Dave kept track of her, a woman "posing" as a friend of the Lovelaces? Should've known she was back in town. Should've known she'd get into trouble. Now, she'd been killed, a woman identified with the proud name of Lovelace, and . . .

"Shocking. Inexcusable. Very bad management, Randall."

Dave took it, squirming and sweating and trying to protest. Finally he escaped—rather he was called out to the desk—and I had a chance to work.

"Obviously" (and let us put that *obviously* in quotes) the two murders—Ellen's and Deborah's—had been committed by the same person. The poems "established" that fact. Certainly two such poems in the possession of two mysteriously murdered women could not be mere coincidence. The man hated them — the hard murderous hate shone through the lines — so . . .

I bore down on the poems so heavily that I almost believed what I said.

"But I don't need to explain all this to you, sir," I said. "You felt that the colonel needed a good jacking up and you took this opportunity of delivering it — of making him sweat a little, if you'll excuse the expression. But you can see that Judge couldn't be guilty. He was in jail at the time of the second murder; therefore he couldn't possibly be guilty of either one. . . . That's your opinion, isn't it, sir? I've stated your own thoughts correctly? You feel that Judge — the *Courier* — is in no way involved in this scandal?"

It was, it appeared, exactly the way he felt. I had stated his own thoughts perfectly, and he complimented me on my astuteness.

"Very — uh — shrewd of you, Brown. Couldn't have put the matter more clearly myself. But this — this Chasen woman —"

"I was coming to that, sir. When you call Detective Stukey about Judge — You were going to do that right away, I suppose? After all, a *Courier* man shouldn't —"

"Certainly!" he snapped. "Demand his immediate release! Can't think what the police department is coming to to make such a ghastly error."

"Well," I went on, "I was thinking you might clarify Mrs. Chasen's position while you were talking to Stukey. We have our duty to the public, sir. We can't allow baseless rumors to get into circulation. As I see it — regardless of her claims — Mrs. Chasen was *not* a friend. She was not even an acquaintance, in the accepted sense of the term. It seems to me, sir, that she was merely another visitor to the building, one of the many sight-seers who come here yearly to—"

"Exactly! That's exactly the case, Mr. Brown. Don't know why I—uh—I'll call Stukey immediately."

He called, and Stukey was far from pleased, from what I could gather. But he didn't have any evidence against Tom, and he hadn't been able to make him talk. And there was no small amount of logic in "Lovelace's" opinion about the connection between the two murders. Moreover—most important, of course, was the fact that Lovelace was Lovelace. You didn't say no to him if you could avoid it.

Stukey had no grounds for avoiding it.

So Tom was promptly released…and fired almost as promptly. Just as soon as he could be reached by phone. He'd not been a very good worker to begin with, and now he'd had the bad judgment to get himself arrested. And—

But we don't need to go this fast. We can slow down a little now.

I talked a while longer, "restating" Mr. Lovelace's thoughts for him. He frowned a trifle, but he was forced to admit that I had voiced them perfectly.

"Uh—yes. Must be done, I suppose. Public duty and all. Of course, the murderer may have left the city—"

"I'm positive he hasn't," I said. "As sure as I'm sitting here, sir, he's still in town."

"Yes—uh—probably. Doubtless. Have to get him, eh? See that this Stukey fellow—uh—keeps out the—uh—dragnet. Continues the clean-up. Right?"

I told him his mind worked like a steel trap. "I don't know

how you do it, sir. I mean, see right through to the point of things."

"You think—*ahem*—you really think I do, Mr. Brown?"

"Like a steel trap," I repeated firmly. . . .

Dave was just heading for Lovelace's office as I came out, and I thought he appeared somewhat chagrined when he learned that everything had been settled without him. Along with the chagrin, however, was considerable relief at getting the old man off his neck. And he seemed pleased at the latter's instructions to fire Tom Judge.

"I should have done it long ago." He nodded. "Just didn't have the heart. Now it's out of my hands."

I started toward my desk. He touched me on the arm. "By the way, Brownie. You spent the better part of a day with Mrs. Chasen. . . ."

"You're right," I said. "It all comes back to me now that you mention it."

"I'm not trying to pry, but—you thought quite a bit of her, didn't you? I got the impression that you were pretty annoyed with Lovelace's references to her."

"I loved her, Colonel," I said. "Her image is permanently graven on my heart. I could have gone for her in a large way— if, unfortunately, I had not lacked certain essential equipment."

He winced, managed a sympathetic smile. "Well, we'll put someone else on this one. You keep out of the office today—go out to the Fort. They're having maneuvers with a lot of VIPs present. You phone in the story—maybe an interview or two if it's convenient—and don't show back here until tomorrow."

I was startled almost to the point of speechlessness. My absence would leave the office seriously undermanned, and

Stukey would certainly want to talk to me. To send me off for the day on a relatively unimportant story was virtually idiocy. Or something.

"You go on," Dave repeated firmly, in answer to my puzzled mumblings. "I've got a guy coming in—used to work on the labor rag here before it folded—and Stukey can wait. He won't know what the hell to do, anyway, and I can probably give him about as much dope on Mrs. Chasen as you can."

"But, Colonel—" I stared at him, frowning, still too stunned for proper speech. "I—I don't believe—"

"I don't want Stukey bothering you. That's one reason I'm getting you out of here. Now, go on and take it easy and—and, look. How about that dinner tonight? Come on out to the house about six, huh?"

I said I would. I wanted to talk to the colonel, outside of the office with its many interruptions. There was a terrible price attached to the privilege, but I believed it would be worth it. Broadly speaking, of course. In actuality, there was no proper compensation for the torture of an evening with Kay Randall.

I drove out to the Fort, leisurely, wondering how, if I ever found the opportunity, I should polish Kay off. The most appropriate way, I felt, would be to hit her with a father. She always called Dave "father" and I think that any wife under sixty who does that should be hit with one.

Again—and this would be especially fitting—she might be drowned in mayonnaise. Kay cooked with mayonnaise; it was her rod and her staff, kitchen-wise. Mayonnaise was to Kay as can opener is to Newlywed. I felt reasonably sure that she had whole hogsheads of the stuff concealed in the cellar. If one could surprise her at just the right moment—catch her while she was dipping out a couple of ten-gallon pails for the evening meal—well...

But probably she had become immune to it; probably she could breathe in it as a fish breathes in water. In any event there were other ways, and all very pleasant to contemplate.

One might ash-tray her to death, for example. You could place her at the end of a vast room while you sat at the other end. And you would be equipped with unlimited cigarettes and a thimble-size ash-tray, and she with a pair of binoculars. Then...well, perhaps your own experience will allow you to imagine the rest. Driven by an insane urge, Kay would have to empty the tray each time you dropped a speck of ash in it. And each time, before returning to her post, she would have to give you a bright little smile and say, "My! You *do* smoke a lot, don't you?" As soon as she returned to her post, of course, you would drop ashes again and Kay would...

No. No, it was nice to think about, but it would never work. Kay had been in training too long. There might be ways of running her to death, but you could never do it with the ash-tray routine.

Probably no one method would be adequate to dispose of her, for that matter. You would have to use a combination of all available means. You might, say, join the several hundred doilies and antimacassars in the living-room into a sack, fill it with mayonnaise, and tie it over Kay's head. Then you could remove her shoes and start dropping ashes on her feet, and Kay—

Hell.

To hell with Kay. How could I think of Kay when Deborah—

But I couldn't think about Deborah either. I was afraid to think about her....

I arrived at the Fort and repaired to the public-relations office. Except for brief intervals, I stayed there until quitting time, sprawled out on a lounge within reaching distance of the bar.

The story wasn't worth my time. The p.r. men could cover it better than I could, and I felt that they should. P.r. men don't work enough. They are always pushing you to take a story, and when you agree they let it slide and come at you with something else. They will give you pictures, yes, possibly some you can use if you are real hard up. They will set up interviews, yes, possibly with someone quite well known in his own neighborhood. But stories, no. They can talk story, but they can never give you one. Some strange psychological quirk keeps them from carrying through.

However, I got them to work, and they produced a fairly good story on the maneuvers as well as two interviews with the VIPs.

"You can do it, men," I said as I swung open the doors of the bar. "You have lingered in the nest too long, and now you must fly. Begone, and do not return without you-know-what. Otherwise, no word anent this occasion shall creep into the *Courier* and your asses shall be ashes."

It was what they needed—firm words and a steely eye. They tottered away, nervous but determined, and they returned triumphant. I called their stuff in to the desk.

At three o'clock I sent in some pictures for overnight and knocked off. I went home and cleaned up, taking no more time about it than I had to. Then I went to a bar and stayed until a quarter of six, when I started for Dave's house.

Until the last six months or so, they had been living in a

comfortable apartment at a surprisingly reasonable rental. But Kay had wanted "a little place of their very own," so they had got this thing. It was little, all right, all bright new paint and shiny doorknobs—and rooms approximately the size of packing crates. But it was a very long way from being theirs. By the time Dave paid off the mortgage, his two "kiddies"—four and six—would be well past the voting age.

Kay *knew* that I wanted to see the "little ones," so I was taken in for a look immediately. And that I could have done without.

The little boy, the oldest, had said a naughty word, it seemed, and the little girl had repeated it after him. Kay beamed down at them primly, commanding them to confess their evil to me.

They confessed, sniffling and rubbing their eyes.

"And Mother had to punish you, didn't she? She had to wash your mouths out with soap."

They admitted it. Also that poor mother had been hurt by the punishment much worse than they.

Well, the poor little devils had got one break anyway. They'd been put to bed without any dinner.

We left, and Kay led me up the hall to the bathroom where she was *sure* I wanted to wash my hands.

"Just my mind," I said. "I've been thinking some naughty thoughts."

"Oh, you! You're so funny, Clint!" She laughed. And her eyes said, *The hell you are, bud!*

We went into the living-room. Kay produced two hand-cut glasses and a bottle of sixty-cent sherry, and gave Dave and me a drink. She waited, standing, poised to snatch the glasses from our hands the moment we were finished.

We did and she did, and dinner was served.

It was mayonnaise and something else, something I couldn't immediately identify. It was served on individual plates of Haviland china.

"Well, Father?" Kay smiled at Dave, firmly. "How do you like it?"

Dave mumbled that it was very good, slanting an apologetic glance at me. "Afraid we should have given you something else, Brownie. You'd probably have preferred a steak."

"Oh, of course, he wouldn't!" Kay laughed. "Clinton can eat steak any time.... How do *you* like it, Clint?"

"I'd like to have the recipe," I said. "I don't believe I've ever eaten rubber gloves prepared in quite this way."

Her eyes flashed, but she went right on laughing. She was a laughing little woman, this Kay. A joyous little mother.

"Silly! You can't tease me, Clinton Brown. It's iced frankfurters in hot mayonnaise-parsnip ring."

"No!" I said. "I don't believe it."

"Mmmm-hmmm. That's what it is."

"Clint—" Dave frowned. "If you don't—"

"Now you just leave Clinton alone, Father. He can speak for himself."

"It's wonderful," I said. "I don't know how you do it, Kay."

She wasn't kidding me any. Not a goddamned bit. There couldn't be such a thing as iced frankfurters in hot mayonnaise-parsnip ring. This was just what I'd thought: rubber gloves in hand lotion with chopped sponge dressing.

I ate quite a bit of the stuff. I'd had almost nothing to eat since Deborah—since the day before, and I was hungry. It was going to make me sick—I could feel the sickness coming on—but I went ahead and ate.

157

Kay brought coffee (an unreasonable facsimile thereof, I should say) and something called Marshmallow Grape Surprise. I wasn't up to any further surprise, nor was Dave apparently, so she ate her dessert alone.

"Oh, Clinton!" she said, lapping up the last bite of the mess. "You didn't get our flowers, did you? I mean, the ones we sent to the funeral."

"Kay —" Dave squirmed.

"Now, Father. I just asked Clinton a simple question. I know he couldn't have got them. We didn't get any card of acknowledgment."

She smiled at me, wide-eyed. I said I couldn't understand why she hadn't got the card. "I sent it registered mail," I said. "Registered with return receipt requested."

"Y-You" — she stammered — "you did?"

"Are you sure the kiddies didn't get hold of it?" I said. "They might have mistaken it for a naughty picture."

"Clint —" said Dave.

I was getting tired. Tired and damned sick.

"I got the flowers," I said, "and thank you very, very much. Thank you for all your kindness, Kay. Incidentally, I hope you weren't disturbed when the police called here that night. I could never forgive myself if you were."

"The police?" Kay looked blank. "The police didn't call here."

"A man named Stukey. He called here trying to locate me."

"Not here, he didn't. I was home all — Oh!" Her face cleared. "Father was at the Chamber of Commerce banquet that night. The answering service must have referred the call there."

"Answering service?" I looked at Dave. "I thought —"

"Mmmm-hmmm," said Kay. "It's awfully convenient for

158

Father when he has to be away from home at night. He just gives them the number of the place where he'll be and they call there direct. Just as though it were his own number. I mean, when this number is dialed they automatically call the other—"

"Very interesting. But suppose it was someone who wanted to talk to you?"

"Oh, I never take any calls in the evening! All my acquaintances know that. I keep my evenings free for Father and the kiddies."

That figured, all right. She could give her undivided attention to making them miserable.

"Of course, it's one more expense and I—well—" She sighed bravely. "Goodness knows we don't have a penny to spare. It seems we're always having company, and.... Well, anyway, I feel that it just can't be avoided with Father away so much. Let's see, where did you have to go last night, Father? The Rotary Club, wasn't it?"

"Uh—yes," Dave muttered, and he lifted his coffee cup.

His hand trembled. His eyes wouldn't meet mine.

There'd been no Rotary Club meeting last night. There'd been no Chamber of Commerce banquet on the night that Ellen was killed.

I pushed back my chair and stood up.

"I'm going to have to go," I said. "I'm—I don't feel very well."

"Oh, no, you're not!" Kay cried gaily. "We're going to keep him right here, aren't we, Father? We're going to keep this big, bad ol' Clinty right here where we can—"

"Sorry," I said, "and thanks for the dinner. I have to go."

I started to turn away from the table. She jumped up and flung her arms around me from the rear, hugging me around the waist.

"Help me, Father! You know what he wants to do. He's going off to some dirty ol' bar, and—"

I brought an elbow back suddenly. She grunted and reeled backward, batting her fat little head against the wall.

"F-Father," she whimpered. "H-He—he!"

"I saw it." Dave was looking at me at last, very white around the mouth. "Get out, Clint. I've put with...I've tried to—to— *Get out!*"

"Out of your house, Father?" I said. "Out of your life? Out of your journalistic sphere? Could you possibly mean that I am fired, Colonel?"

"Clint! I'm asking you to—"

"I thought you were telling me," I said. "Am I fired, Colonel?"

"Yes!" he yelled. "Yes! Now—get—out!"

I got out. I couldn't have stayed another minute if I'd been paid to.

I headed for the car, half-doubled over, a thousand hot knives twisting in my stomach. I started vomiting, and I am an old hand at that game, a charter member of the Heave-It League, but this was in a class by itself.

I drove homeward, my head necessarily out the window all the way, and I was going as strong when I got there as when I had started. There wasn't anything in me, but the heaving went right on.

I uncorked a bottle and upended it into my mouth. The stuff wasn't halfway down before it started bouncing. I choked and made another try. The same thing happened—and more.

A great hand seemed to grab me in the guts and squeeze. The bottle fell from my hands. I fell to the floor, writhing.

That one passed, that convulsion. But there were indications that others were on the way. I staggered into the bedroom, jerked open the bureau drawers. I knew what I had to do, but there was something else I had to do first. Get into some pajamas. A pair with all the buttons and no holes. Even then there was a chance that they might see, but—

But I had to risk it. I knew I'd die if I didn't.

I was struggling to get my pants over the pajamas when Stukey arrived. He gave me one startled glance. Then, with none of the questions asked which he had doubtless come to ask, he started helping me with the pants.

"Jesus, keed!" he panted. "Come on! Let the screwin' clothes go. I'll take you in my car, open up the siren. You got any particular place in mind?"

"Any of them," I said. "Any hospital."

"Jesus!" He pulled my arm around his shoulders, lugged me toward the door. "When'd it hit you, pal? What done it?"

"I—rubber gloves," I said. "An original recipe."

" 'At's the ol' keed, the Brownie boy," he said. "Pile it in, pal."

16

As you have probably guessed, it was a case of acute food poisoning, one of the more painful and dangerous kinds since it was the result of spoiled meat. The franks had had pork in them, and bad pork can be deadly. Fortunately, I'd expelled the stuff quickly, and I'd wasted no time in getting to the hospital, where my stomach was washed and penicillin administered. Such crisis as may have existed was over within an hour or so. My insides were sore as a blister and I hardly had the strength to raise a hand, but I was out of danger.

I was in the hospital two days — very dreary ones, since the authorities made drinking difficult for me and sometimes impossible. There was little to do except lie there and think, endlessly, unproductively, unpleasantly, to chase myself around and around in that unbroken, seamless circle.

Kay...well, of course, she'd done it deliberately. I'd had a standing dinner invitation for weeks, and she'd known that I'd come eventually. So a few franks — just enough for me — had been allowed to spoil, and, their rottenness disguised with more slop, I'd eaten them. Yes, she must have done it deliberately, or so I believed — and I will admit to some slight prejudice where

Kay is concerned. But just what her motivation had been, I was not sure. Was it merely some more of her sheer orneriness, a typical Kay Randall stunt? Had the little woman only been demonstrating that regardless of poor ol' softie-Father's feelings, *she* had no use for me and I'd better behave if I didn't want to catch what-for?

That was probably the case. And to be fair to her—a painful necessity—she probably had had no intention of killing me. Dave told her everything, practically, or, rather, she wormed everything out of him in long jolly evenings beside the mayonnaise bowl. She would sit him down amid the antimacassars and pull his sweet ol' funny head into the environs of her cute little old belly button, and then Father would simply have to tell her what was on his mind. She would be very hurt if he did not; she would be afraid he didn't love her any more. And when Kay felt that way—as Father well knew—the aforesaid environs went out of bounds. There were no larksome expeditions thereto, nor invasions thereof, nor maneuvers thereon. So Father, who was already yearning for a brisk patrol with a barrage at the end, would tell all (approximately). He would say, *"Well, it's Brownie, dammit. I don't mind, personally, but I'm afraid Mr. Lovelace will..."* And Kay's eyes would grow moist and her mind murderous, and she would say, *"Oh, how awful. Perhaps if we showed more interest in Clinton, invited him out for a good home-cooked meal...."*

Exit Father and Mother to bedroom. Enter frankfurters, parsnips, mayonnaise, and Clinton Brown.

That must have been the deal. Kay had given Clint a lesson, and Clint would know that he had had one. He—I—would

163

know that the poisoning had been intentional, and take the hint. I was to lay off of Father or else.

So...

But there was Tom Judge, what he had told me. And there was the fact that Dave had been away from home on those two nights, that he had lied about his whereabouts and let me think, at least in the instance of Ellen, that he *had* been at home. Then there was that reef connecting the mainland and the island, and a lone taxicab crossing the border. And...and most of all there was Deborah, that strange feeling I'd had about her, that I could never have...

Did I say yes? Did I say that it did make sense? I did not. I didn't pretend to know what it all meant—if it meant anything. Nevertheless it existed, so much to be explained, and I *had* been poisoned. I had almost been killed.

I went round and round the circle, thinking, trying to look into myself, where the clue to the mystery probably lay. What had I overlooked, what small factor, that kept me from seeing what I should see?

I didn't know. I don't know now—now, when this manuscript is approximately two thirds finished and its pages flow higgledy-piggledy over my desk. *(And has someone crept into the room? Is someone lurking in the shadows behind me, trying to read what I have written?)*

But I can tell you this, my good friends—oh, yes, and you sorry ignominious foes—I have a strong hunch that I *will* know before it comes time to type # # # or—30—. And my hunch tells me that I will be quite as much surprised as you are.

Now, perhaps a few words about the doctor are in order.

I had slept almost none at all the first night, but promptly at seven o'clock a nurse came in and induced me to wash and presented me with a breakfast tray. She was a grimly prim little person, unpleasantly reminiscent of Kay Randall. She crisply advised me that I was to partake of the food at once and that it would do me a lot of good (an obvious and preposterous falsehood). I replied that it was just such victuals as these that had put me where I was and that the burned child shuns the fire.

We were discussing the matter, i.e., the digestibility of cold oatmeal, skim milk, and stale toast, when the doctor came in. He told the nurse to leave the tray; I could eat or go hungry, just as I pleased. She left, and without preliminary he asked me how much whisky I drank a day. I replied that I never kept track of it.

"You'd better start in," he said curtly. "The amount of alcohol in your bloodstream now would be lethal for the average person. I can't answer for the results if you keep on going as you've been doing."

"That's fair enough," I said. "After all, I don't believe I consulted you in the matter. May I ask a question, Doctor?"

He nodded, flushing, an angry glint in his eye. "If you make it snappy."

"It's a question that's frequently arisen in my mind when coming in contact with the medical profession. Briefly, if treating the sick annoys you so much, why don't you get into another racket?"

"All right" — he turned on his heel — "I've warned you. And I'm telling you this, too. You'll do no drinking while you're here. You can crack up and go into d.t.'s, that's up to you. But you won't do it in this hospital."

He stalked out righteously, a true-blue man of mercy, a man who took no nonsense from the people who paid him. Around nine o'clock in the morning, Stukey arrived.

I thanked him for his help the night before. I demanded the pint which I felt sure was responsible for the bulge in his coat.

"Well, look, keed." He hesitated. "They told me downstairs that—"

"They are insane," I said. "Feeble-minded. A few of the worst mental cases, allowed to play hospital as occupational therapy. My word on it, Stuke, also my hand. Place the pint in it."

"Yeah, but—pal. If it's going to—"

"Did it ever? Have I ever been noticeably affected by it? Give, my friend."

He gave it to me, watching the door anxiously as I drank. I had a small one—no more than a third, at most—and tucked the bottle under my pillow.

"Now," I said. "Now, you will have some questions."

"Yeah," he nodded tiredly, "I guess. Goddammit to hell, anyway."

He didn't get down to the questions immediately. He was sore about having to let Tom Judge go, and the dragnet wasn't producing anything, and he knew it wasn't going to (nothing but a reduction in his graft). And he was completely baffled as to how to proceed.

I told him to keep a high heart; honest effort was never lost. If nothing else resulted from the investigation, we would at least have a clean city.

"Yeah." He looked at me oddly. "A lot of fun, ain't it?"

"We-ell," I said, "I do believe there are slight overtones of humor."

"Uh-huh, sure. Real funny, all right. I try to be a pal to you, an'—"

"Perhaps I can be one to you," I said. "I was down to Mexico the other day, and I learned about a reef—"

"I know all about it. Hell, there was waves running ten feet high over the damned thing. A guy tried to cross that, and he'd've wound up in Key West."

"Still, it's within the realm of possibility," I said.

"That realm I don't know nothing about. Maybe they got a bay up there, too, and a guy who could've swum across it in the storm."

"Is that an innuendo, Stuke? Are you returning to your original evil suspicions?"

He grinned sheepishly and shook his head. "Lay off, will you? How many times I got to apologize? I was sore and I wasn't thinkin' straight and—well, to hell with it. What d'you know about this Mrs. Chasen?"

"Something special," I said. "Something extra special, Stuke. I wanted to bring her down to the police station that day, but she wouldn't go. Afraid you'd want to fingerprint her, I believe—very broadly speaking—and her rear end was tender from previous attempts."

"No foolin', keed. Where—"

"I drove her around for the better part of a day. I fed her lunch, booze, and put her on the train."

"You took her out to the dog pound."

"And back. With many a pleasant way stop along the lonely route. As I say, Stuke, she was quite a dish. A wonderful partner in the ancient and honorable pastime of parking."

He sat staring at me steadily for a second. He frowned and said, "Yeah, but, keed—" Then he shrugged and went on: "You know she was supposed to take a boat to Europe? Well, how come she didn't instead of hangin' around L.A.?"

"Doubtless she was in love with me," I said. "She couldn't leave California as long as I was in it. Of course, we'd only known one another for less than a day, but—"

"Cut it out, Brownie. What'd she say when you saw her in L.A.?"

"Now now, Stuke. Puh-lease!"

"Okay, so you didn't see her. Didn't talk to her either, I suppose?"

"I did not," I said. "The record of her call to the Press Club is an outrageous forgery, one more link in a Communist plan to do me in."

Stukey grinned reluctantly. "No offense, keed. Just habit. I even try to trip myself up. What'd she call you about?"

"About Ellen. You know, to say that she was sorry and so on."

"Yeah? What else?"

"Oh, just to say that she loved me and there could never be another man in her life and—"

"Always clownin'." He sighed. "She didn't mention any other guy? Someone that could have brought her back here, or she might've come back here to see?"

"No, she didn't. As I mentioned a moment ago, there could be no other man where she was concerned."

"Keed," he said. "I'm beggin' you. Be serious, huh? This thing has got me runnin' in circles. The autopsy—well, maybe it wouldn't have told us nothin', anyway, but even that nothin'

would have been some help. We could've found out what
didn't happen to her, if we'd had anything halfway like a
corpus, an'—an' it's all like that, keed! Just nothin' to work on.
There's fifty buses into here a day and six trains and four air-
plane flights, an' how the hell you goin' to know when she got
here or whether she came alone or...or what? I'm telling you.
Let me tell you how it stands. I got a couple of pretty good
pictures of her from her home-town paper, and we duped a
batch and showed 'em around. Well. Up to date we got her
placed on eight buses and one train and there's a truck driver
that swears she tried to thumb a ride out of Long Beach
with him."

I opened the bottle and had another drink. I offered him my
deepest sympathy. "Just keep striving, Stuke," I said. "Your head
in the clouds and your feet on the ground."

"I'm laughin'," he said. "It's funny as hell, this is. On top of
everything else I got those bollixing poems. All the something I
got is something to screw me up."

"You don't think they're a clue?" I said.

"Clues, schmooz. Sure, they're a clue and what the hell you
goin' to do with it? The guy's got a head on him, he's sharp like
tacks, he ain't a money killer. That's your clue, an' you can buy it
cheap. It ain't givin' me nothing but ulcers."

"Terrible," I said. "Now, wait a minute, Stuke. I'm not
laugh—"

"Well"—he shrugged and stood up—"I wish I could. Why'n't
you kill that jug, so's I can take it with me."

I took the last drink and handed him the bottle. He trudged
out drearily, his snappy hat pulled low over his eyes, a pronounced
sag in the shoulders of his suit.

I was a little ashamed for having laughed at him, and I'd honestly tried not to. But I hadn't been able to help it. Poor Stuke, lord of the pimps and bookies, terror of the panhandlers — Stukey, stripped of his last penny of graft and with no prospects but hard work. No graft, no glory. Nothing but having to earn his salary if he hoped to keep drawing it.

Poor Lem. I couldn't help laughing, pathetic as he was.

He returned that night with another pint, and the next morning, ditto. Not officially. It wasn't business, keed, he said. He just happened to be out this way and figured I could use a little company.

He came out Saturday morning and drove me home, and he remained to visit there, with rather startling, even alarming, results. You see, I was getting just a little weary of him. I had had several hours of his moaning and groaning in a mere forty-eight, and —

But let's move back a bit. Back to the hospital and Thursday.

Stukey didn't know about my trouble with Dave, so, as a friendly act, he'd left word of my illness at the office. He hadn't talked with Dave, just the switchboard operator. But I knew that Dave would be informed as soon as he arrived at work, and I was frankly worried when he didn't call.

It was just possible that he *had* fired me, that he intended to make it stick, or try to. And I knew what would happen if he did. Lovelace was already a little down on Dave just as he was very much up on me. He'd never let Dave fire me. He'd insist that I be taken back. Moreover, he'd credit Dave with one more error in judgment, one more than Dave could comfortably stand.

And if Dave got stubborn, he'd be fired himself.

I didn't want that. I didn't want his position made so shaky that he might fall out of it. Not yet, anyway. *Status quo*—with, naturally, reasonable deviations: that would do me for the present.

It was almost noon before he did call. But the delay was not, it developed, due to stubbornness or a last-ditch struggle with Lovelace. It was just that he had difficult and embarrassing things to say, and he had put off saying them as long as possible.

"Brownie," he began, "I—are you all right? I m-meant to call you earlier, but I thought you might be asleep, and the nurse said you were fine."

"A true conservative," I said. "I hope her noncommittal prognosis didn't upset you?"

"Brownie. Look, fellow—"

"As a matter of fact, Colonel, I am doing as well as could be expected. A little light in the abdominal area, but then I have been for several years. One of those things, you know, or rather the absence of one of those things. I—yes, Colonel?"

"About last night, Brownie. I—that was all my fault. You were deathly sick, and she—we tried to prevent you from leaving. I'm sorry, and I'm sure you're sorry. Why don't we just say the whole thing never happened?"

"All of it? The climactic scene where we faced one another across the Marshmallow Grape Surprise, our stomachs growling in agony and bitter frankfurter-flavored burps on our lips?"

"Brownie"—he laughed nervously—"I...well, of course, you know you aren't fired. I'd never have said it if—if you hadn't practically forced me to. I'm not saying that I wasn't at fault, too, but—"

"Let's just lay it to mayonnaise nerves," I said. "I'll be ready to return to work Monday, Colonel, according to the latest dispatch. So if you're positive you didn't mean it—"

"Of course I didn't mean it! My God, Brownie, how could we break up after all the years we've been together? I"—he hesitated and cleared his throat—"I *have* tried to be a friend, Brownie. I—I know how you feel about that—the accident, and I've tried to make up for it the best I could. I...Look. Will you do me a very great favor?"

"Such as eating a nice home-cooked meal? Practically anything but that, Colonel."

"It's about Lovelace. What I want you to tell him about... about why you're off work."

"Yes?" I said. And suddenly I was frowning. "Just what am I supposed to tell him?"

"I had to do it, Brownie! I"—his voice broke, and picked up again, shamed, embarrassed—"I...maybe it wasn't necessary, but I was afraid to take the chance. You know how he's been toward me lately. And he—he and his wife have been down on Kay ever since—well, you can guess. They spent an evening with us, too. I just couldn't risk it, Clint. I'm head over heels in debt and—"

"Let's have it, Colonel," I said. "I didn't damned near die of rotten meat served up by the Mayonnaise Queen, so what is the ailment that keeps me from work at a time when I'm badly needed? Creeping clap? Too much marijuana? A slight case of—"

"Please, Clint! Don't make me feel any cheaper than I do already."

"Tell me," I said, "And tell me what I do if Lovelace decides to check up."

"He won't. I told him it was nothing serious, but you were supposed to have absolute rest for a few days. That's not too far from the truth, is it, Brownie? You do need a rest. You've been under a terrific emotional strain."

"Old Reporters' Home," I said, "roll wide your doors and trundle out the straitjacket. Here comes Brownie."

"All right, Clint. Have your own way about it. If you don't know me well enough by this time to—"

"Oh, I do, Colonel," I said. "I don't doubt your motives in the slightest. Until Monday, then, eh, when I shall stagger wan and wild-eyed into the *Courier* city room."

"Clint. I wish you didn't feel—"

"So do I," I said. "And a very good morning to you, Colonel."

I hung up. I dug under the pillow for the bottle before I remembered that it wasn't there.

Well, I didn't have to have a drink. I could use one, but I didn't have to have it. My hand wandered under the pillow again, and I jerked it back with a suddenness that set the fingers to tingling.

Damn the bottle. Damn Dave. Yes, and a double-damn for Clinton Brown. Dave couldn't hurt me with Lovelace. He hadn't tried to get me in trouble, only to keep himself out of it. But still, I wished he hadn't done this.

It didn't mean anything. That answering-service deal didn't

173

mean anything. Nor the reef, nor the cab across the border, nor — None of them meant a thing, by itself.

But when you put them all together...?

Meaningless even then. They still added up to nothing that I could see.

But I wished he hadn't done this.

17

I was half-starved by Saturday morning, and I made the mistake of saying so as Lem Stukey drove me home.

He knew exactly what I needed, Stuke did. It seemed that his middle name was Grub, he was a chow hound from way back. His old lady, his mother, had taught him how to cook—when she wasn't busy droppin' another kid—and he was kinda hungry himself. He'd been screwing around on this case for goddamned near twenty-four hours straight, and some chow would fit right into the old spot.

It was no trouble at all, keed. Honest. We was pals, wasn't we, and he wanted to eat himself. Anyway, he didn't have a thing to do. He was already half nuts from this screwy deal, and he was going to have to pull out a while. Jesus, a guy couldn't keep goin' night and day, could he? A guy was entitled to eat, wasn't he?

And he wasn't gettin' nowhere nohow. Just puttin' out, and not gettin' a goddamned thing back.

We got to the house, and he lugged the stuff he'd bought into the kitchen. I wasn't to do a thing, he insisted. I was to park it and let it rest, and he'd take care of everything.

He hung his coat over the back of a chair, tucked an apron

into the belt of his high-waisted pants, and rolled up the sleeves
of his striped silk shirt. I lingered a moment, watching him. He
studied the various packages, his hands absently stroking his
oily black hair. Then he nodded, deciding to begin with the
steaks. He unwrapped them, and his polished nails trailed over
them lovingly.

"Ain't that something, keed? You ever—What's the matter,
pal? You don't like 'em?"

"They look wonderful," I said. "I was just reminded suddenly
that I was out of salad oil."

"Not now you ain't. I got some. I got everything we need,
keed, so you just park it and leave the chow to me."

I went into the living room, taking a bottle with me. I
parked it.

I was being needlessly finicky, I supposed. That was probably
salad oil on Lem's hair, entirely edible and harmless. As for the
nail polish, well, it would cook off. The fire would take care
of it.

I called that I was going to take a bath, and Lem called back
to go right ahead. There was plenty of time. You tried to hurry
good chow and you'd screw it up sure as hell.

I wished he wouldn't use that word—at least in connection
with food. More than that, I wished he'd clear out. I wondered
why he was hanging around.

I took a quick cold shower, necessarily having to dress and
undress in the bathroom. I got the cuffs of my pants wet, and
they clung irritatingly around my ankles. I began to feel a little
toward Stuke as I felt toward Kay Randall.

I went back to the living-room and picked up the bottle.

We ate in there, the living-room, my food on the coffee table,

Stuke's on one of the kitchen chairs with another chair pulled up in front of it.

It was very good. I forgot all about the hair oil and the nail polish. Almost all about it. I ate, stealing a glance now and then at Stukey. He was tackling the food with both hands, stuffing it down. Eating as though it might be snatched away from him. It made me wince a little to watch him. I felt a faint twinge of sickness that was not entirely of the stomach.

"You mentioned your mother a while ago," I said. "Something about your family. You came from a large one?"

"Well"—he gulped, swallowed, and stabbed another piece of steak—"kind of. Six boys and three girls. Yeah"—gulp—"they was nine of us, one right behind the other. They used to call us the stairsteps over at the ol' sixth-ward school."

"You mean...you mean this is your home, where you were born?" I don't know why I was startled by this idea. "Somehow, I—"

"Yeah? Yeah, we was all born and raised here. Not the old folks, y'know, but all us kids was. All livin' here right now."

"No," I said. "No, they are not, Stukey. And I say that as a close student of the city payroll."

He choked on a mouthful of salad. Chuckled. "You—Off the record, keed?"

"Off the record."

"Well, you look for Stowe sometime. Or Sutton. Or Sutke or—le's see. I guess that's about the crop, countin' the two Stowes. The girls is married and don't hold jobs." He forked more steak and stacked salad on top of it. He nodded to me seriously. "There's nothin' crooked about it, you understand. O' course, I got 'em all in with the city, but there ain't nothin' funny about the names. We just couldn't use the other, see, and we kind of switched it around to suit ourselves. You ever hear of a goddamned name with two z's and an x in it?"

I said I had been spared that. "Your parents. Are they still living?"

"Yeah, they're still around. I—You didn't know that? I thought you knew I lived with 'em.... Kind of funny, ain't it? I mean, you see a guy day in and day out, and it comes up you don't know hardly nothin' about him."

"Yes," I said. "Yes, that is strange, Stuke."

"Yeah, I got a couple acres out on West Road. Gives the old man some place to screw around. He never had no trade, y'see. He was a farmer in the old country, and about all he could do over here was yard work. Spading up gardens an' mowing lawns an' trimming hedges and stuff like that. He—" Stukey swallowed and laughed suddenly. "Jesus, I just remembered something."

"Yes?" I said. "Share it with me, Stuke."

"Sure." His eyes brimmed with laughter. "I wonder what in the hell made me think of it. Why, Christ, it must've been almost thirty years ago. I was—yeah—I was just about seven, an'—or was it eight? Well, anyway. The old man was working on a place out in Hacienda Hills, an' this dame—the lady of the house—finds herself short a diamond brooch. She'd just misplaced the damn thing, you know, and she found it the same day. But meanwhile she just knows the old man hooked it, and she calls the cops on him. An'—*ha, ha*—Jesus, keed—*ha, ha, ha, ha*..."

He paused and brushed the tears from his eyes. He went on: "He couldn't talk English, see? Just maybe a few words. He didn't know what it was all about an' he was scared as hell, naturally, and all he could think of to do was keep his mouth shut. Well—*ha, ha*—you know how that would sit with the cops. They dragged him out in the garage of this place, and they took turns workin' on him. Hit him with everything they could lay hands on. Hoehandles, rakes, spades, every goddamned thing. If that dame hadn't found her brooch an hour later, they'd've broken every hand tool on the place.... You never seen nothin' like it, Clint; the old man was black and blue for the next three months."

"And that's funny?" I said. "You can laugh about that?"

"Cryin's better? What the hell, the old man thought it was a good joke, too. But I ain't told you all of it.... The cops was kind of worried an' sorry about makin' the mistake, so they brought him out to the house and helped the old lady put him to bed. They were pretty good guys, it turned out. Kind of tough and stupid maybe, but they wasn't makin' no one trouble just for the hell of it. They turned out their pockets before they left, gave the old man every nickel they had. Came to almost four bucks in all."

I set my coffee cup down and leaned forward on the lounge. "Stuke," I said. "Lem. How in the name of God, just how, with an example like that before you, can you be like you are?"

"I don't dig you, keed." A puzzled frown wrinkled his forehead. "How you mean? What example?"

"Let it go," I said. "What could I mean? They gave your father four bucks, and that was that. That fixed up everything."

"Yeah, it kind of did." Stuke nodded. "The old man took the dough and started to night school. Learned to talk English real good."

179

I couldn't say why I was annoyed by the story. I couldn't say, for that matter, that the story was the source of my annoyance. Probably it was Stukey. I was tired and drowsy. I had much on my mind. I wanted to be alone, and there seemed to be no immediate prospect of that. He showed no signs of leaving.

He sat with his chair tilted back against the wall, the pointed toes of his shoes hooked through the rungs. He was looking down at the food plates, frowning thoughtfully, and picking at his teeth, with a match.

He raised his eyes slowly, letting them come to rest on me. He stared at me, frowning, so deep in thought, apparently, that he was unaware of his stare.

He must have studied me for several minutes, the small bright eyes never shifting from my face. I coughed and cleared my throat, and he gave a little start. But he continued to look at me, and his frown deepened.

"Look, Brownie, what's it all about, anyhow?"

"A very good question," I said, "but I'm afraid I can't give you the answer, offhand. I suggest that you consult an encyclopedia — the A to Z section."

"Why, keed? Why you doin' it to me? We ain't goin' to pull this guy in in no dragnet. You know we ain't. All this — all it's gettin' is me."

"Not solely," I said.

"So? So we're gettin' rid of the hustlers and fast boys. We're cleanin' things up. What does that mean to you?"

"That," I said, "would probably be impossible for you to understand, my friend. I'm not implying, of course, that you are not a highly sentient and understanding soul. I wouldn't think of doing that, old pals that we are."

He grinned feebly, letting the chair legs down to the floor. "Always clownin'," he grumbled. "All the time clownin'.... Just the same, keed, why'n't you give it a rest? It ain't doin' you no good, if you ask me. It's gettin' to where you don't seem to feel right no more unless you're—"

"Yes?" I said, for he had abruptly cut off the sentence, and there was a trace of furtiveness about him. "You were about to say?"

"Nothin'." He shrugged. "What's the difference? I got two murders on my hands, I couldn't lay off of 'em even if you wasn't pokin' at me."

"But you'd much sooner I wouldn't poke, wouldn't you?" I said. "You could be much more leisurely about your investigation. And you could drop it at your own convenience."

"Well—" He began another shrug, then looked at me in sudden alarm. "Now, wait a *min*-ute, keed. That ain't very nice, is it? You make it sound like—like—"

The tiredness and drowsiness had dropped from me like a robe. I was still irritated with him, but I was no longer in any hurry to have him leave. "I was just thinking," I said, "about Ellen. Wondering about her. Do you suppose someone had her come back here—sent her the money to come on?"

"I—how you mean? Who'd want to do that?"

"Who, indeed? But it should be easy to find out, don't you think? The person wouldn't have sent her cash; at least, I don't believe he would. And I doubt very much if he'd've sent anything as potentially incriminating as a check. So that leaves us money orders, records of which, naturally, should be readily available to us.... Why don't you look into them? Or would you like to have me do it?"

"That"—he hesitated—"that wouldn't prove nothin'. Just because he sent her some dough."

"We-ell," I said, "I think it might, Stuke. Particularly if he didn't have a satisfactory explanation for his whereabouts at the time of the murder or murders."

"Maybe he couldn't give no good alibi without foulin' himself up. Maybe he was bedded down with a doll or something like that. Maybe"—his tongue flicked over his lips—"maybe the people who could alibi for him are sore at him now. He might've had to push 'em around since then, and they'd like to see him stuck."

I leaned back against the wall, folding my hands behind my head. "But you agree that she might have been sent some money by one of our local residents? Why do you suppose he did it, Stuke?"

"What's the difference? What if I told—could tell you? You wouldn't believe me."

"Oh, come, now," I said. "You mean one old pal wouldn't believe another old pal? Why don't you—"

"I'll tell you," he said. "I'll tell you this, Brownie. You're going to forget all about anyone sendin' her a money order. You ain't going to nose around them money-order records a goddamned bit. You been pushin' me all over the map, keed, and I been takin' it an' it kind of looks like I got to keep on takin' it for a while. But this way—huh-uh. We don't go no further in this direction."

He had moved over in front of me, as he talked, and now he was looking straight down into my face. He didn't appear threatening, only intensely, deadly serious.

"I'm going to drop it, eh?" I said. "Just what makes you so sure of that, Stuke?"

"I got a couple of reasons. For one thing, you know damned well I didn't kill her, her or the other dame. I didn't have no cause to. It wouldn't have made me nothin'. Huh-uh, Brownie. I ain't killed anyone, and you know I ain't. You can dig me into this deal an' make me look pretty bad. You can turn on the heat until I start stinkin' and they toss me on the dump. But you won't be doin' it because you think I'm the killer."

"And your second reason? The remaining half of the why I am not going to nose around those money-order records a god-damned bit?"

"Why don't we let it lay, keed? Let's skip that one."

"Let's not," I said.

"Okay. I'm tellin' you. You start pushin' me on this frammis an' I'll make you the saddest, sorriest son-of-a-bitch on the West Coast. I wouldn't want to, understand. I'd maybe screw myself by doin' it. But I'd be gettin' it anyway, so that wouldn't matter. Lay off of it, Brownie; don't do no more pushin' on it. Because the old crap will fly and most of it'll be yours."

Well . . .

He sounded like he meant it. It was just possible that, sufficiently aroused, he could carry the threat out. He was a resourceful man when he chose to be, and he had connections in various shady places.

Of prime consideration, of course, was my knowledge that he hadn't committed the murders. Not only because I had, but because they would have got him nothing. Stukey did not do things which got him nothing.

There was no point, then, at least for the present, in pursuing the matter. There was no point in forcing him out of his job. I didn't want him to lose it. As with Dave, the *status quo* suited me fine.

"Lem," I said, "this has been a very nice morning. Good whiskey, inspired food, and intriguing conversation. Two old pals, eating and drinking together, baring their souls in long significant silences and occasional muted bursts of profanity. I think I shall let you ride a while, Lem. 'Twere obscene to do otherwise. Amid such beatitude, the smallest flaw would loom as hideously large as a shotgun at a wedding."

"The keed." He grinned. "You want I should wash up these dishes, Brownie?"

18

The *status quo* continued—with almost indiscernible deviations. Dave was his usual jumpy, worried-sick self. Or more so.
Lovelace was his normal, dim-witted self—or more so. And
Stukey, of course, remained Stukey. I was still his old pal, the
keed, and this goddamned clean-up was killin' him and he was
gettin' nowhere fast on them goddamned murders.... There
was just nothin' to go on, keed. Nothin' but nothin'.

Stories about the murders and the consequent manhunt
became fewer and shorter. Even the big Los Angeles papers,
with unlimited space to fill, began making it a second-section
item.

The emptiness... that continued, too. Only broadening now,
widening, spreading its deadening atmosphere farther and farther, until as far as one could see there was nothing but desert,
parched and withered and lifeless, where a dead man walked
through eternity.

The two-way pull... that did not continue. It lay dormant
within me, of course, awaiting summons. But there was no
urgency for the present, and so for all practical purposes it did
not exist. Somehow that made the emptiness worse. There was
no relief from it, no excursions into that strange outer world

where all things moved at a tangent. I was tied to this world...
and the emptiness. The shack represented something absolutely
essential to me, though completely undefinable. I had to stay
there, and...And she had been there. I couldn't leave the place
where she had been. I couldn't disturb it. The lounge where
she had sat, the stove where she had cooked, the bed where she
had lain.

Nothing could be changed. Everything must remain as
it was.

It was strange how much she had meant to me, and still
meant to me. So much, much more than Ellen had, although I
had known Deborah for a total of hardly two days. I don't mean
that I hadn't loved Ellen or that I wasn't sorry about her. But I
had loved Deborah in a different way, and I was sorry about her
in a different way.

I suppose...Well, it may have been because of Deborah's
admitted and undebatable need for me. She needed me, and no
one but me could fill that need. I did not feel that Ellen had
needed me. She insisted that she did, childishly and stubbornly,
but I was confident that she didn't. I had always felt that I bored
Ellen a little, that she resented my modest mental attributes. I
was certain that, if she chose to, she could have been much happier with someone else.

Deborah...

How could I have done it, merely to — to — win a game?

...I ran into Tom Judge a couple of times.

The first instance was about a week after his release from jail.
He advised me that he was "chief rewrite man" on the Pacific
City *Neighborhood News*. He was doing all right, by God. He
was pulling down a hell of a lot more than he'd ever got on that

lousy *Courier,* and I could tell that to Lovelace the first time I saw him.

I congratulated him and promised to deliver the message. I walked on, considerably depressed. The *Neighborhood News* was printed in a job shop. It was circulated free once-a-week, providing the publisher sold enough advertising to make its issuance worthwhile.

The second time I saw him was something more than two weeks later, the same day I heard from Constance Wakefield (of whom much more and soon).

The *News* publisher, it appeared, had tried to get smart with Tom, and Tom had told him where to get off. Tom didn't take any guff from anyone, a fact which—as he pointed out—I knew as well as he did. He didn't *have* to take any guff; maybe some guys did, but he sure as hell didn't. He was now working as an ACCOUNT EXECUTIVE (capitals, please) for a radio station...and could I let him have a ten-spot? Just until the ol' commissions started rolling?

I gave him twenty.

I returned to the office and went to work on the copy for *Around the Town With Clinton Brown*. Thinking about Tom. Feeling that I should do something to help him.

I can't honestly say that I wanted to help him. I had never liked him—and I still didn't—and I had missed few opportunities to give him the needle. Tom and the needle were made for each other. One could not, at least I could not, see the first without seeking the second. Apart, their situation seemed abnormal and there was an irresistible urge to set it aright. They were natural inseparables, like lead and zinc or Kay and mayonnaise.

Still, despite my dislike for him, I wished there was some way of getting him back on the *Courier*. I was at least indirectly responsible for his discharge, and, strange as it may seem, I rather missed him.

But there was no way I could think of. And if I did manage to get him reinstated he probably wouldn't last long. It was too bad, but it was that way, so that's the way it was.

My phone rang. A straight call from the outside, since there was no accompanying "Hey, Brownie," from the city desk.

I picked up a pencil, lifted the headset from the receiver hook, and said, "Brown, *Courier*."

"How do you do, Mr. Brown," said a reedy but somehow resonant voice. "This is Constance Wakefield."

"Miss? . . . Yes, Miss Wakefield."

"You may have heard of my — our books, Mr. Brown. I am the owner-editor of Wakefield House, the Los Angeles publishers. I have — "

"I'll tell you, Miss Wakefield," I said. "I believe the Brown you want is in our advertising department. If you'll just hold on a — "

"I wanted Mr. Clinton Brown. That's you, isn't it?"

"Yes, but I'm afraid — "

"It's concerning a manuscript of yours. A collection of poems."

The pencil slid from my fingers. I picked it up again, slowly turning it end over end.

"Miss Wakefield," I said. "Did you say — ?"

"Your wife left it with me, Mr. Brown. That is to say, your late wife."

19

Constance Wakefield....

Age about forty. Height about five feet eight. Weight about one hundred and five.

She was all long, bony legs and long, thin, bony wrists and hands. One of those straight-up-and-down women, reminiscent of a stovepipe in almost every detail but warmth. Erect. Aloof. Sallow. Nearsighted and asthmatic.

Constance Wakefield.

I don't have her catalogued yet, and I doubt that I ever will. I can't say, positively, whether she was merely greedy and naïve or an outright blackmailer. Probably...but, no, I don't think I shall make even a qualified declaration on this point. Our talk was hedged about so much that any conclusion would be largely surmise.

I can say that whatever her intentions were, they boded very serious danger for me. Also that the subsidy publishing business—wherein hopeful amateurs are induced to pay for the publication of their work—is riddled with racketeers.

There was a convention in Pacific City that week—some fraternal order, I believe—and the lobby of her hotel was packed. I pushed my way through it to the stairs, mounted them to the fourth floor, and was admitted to her room.

I didn't think I'd attracted any attention, nor would it matter greatly if I had. I look in on all conventions in the interests of the *Courier*. I could have been doing that.

So that was one risk taken care of. As for her telephone call to the *Courier*, well, that, I was very glad to hear, had not been made from her room. She'd been looking forward so much to meeting me—she said. (And she said it almost as soon as I stepped through the door.) So she'd called me from the lobby, from a booth, immediately after registering; she simply couldn't wait until she got upstairs. And—a pale smirk—wasn't that terrible of her?

We sat down, and she fumbled a cigarette into a long imitation-ivory holder. I leaned forward with a match and she jerked away, startled. Then she accepted the light quickly and drew away again.

She wore two pair of glasses, one over the other. She peered at me through them, her eyes bulging behind the lenses like watery oysters. "I—I've had your manuscript for some time, Mr. Brown." She coughed and wiped her lips with a yellowish hand-kerchief. "It's not something that one could publish without a great deal of thought."

"No," I said, "I don't imagine it would be."

"My first decision was to return it to your wife. In fact, I called her and asked that she come in and pick it up. But she never came, and when I called again she'd moved from that address, so"—another smirk, rather nervous—"I held on to it."

"That was very considerate of you," I said. "You'd have been justified in throwing it away."

The oysters squirmed slightly. I gave them a pleasant smile.

"Well—uh—of course, I couldn't have done that, Mr. Brown. Manuscripts are precious things. Always entitled to respect and conscientious treatment, regardless of one's approval or disapproval."

"I see," I said. "Am I correct in assuming, Miss Wakefield, that you wish to publish those poems?"

"Well, uh, naturally they would have to have a great deal of editing."

"Yes," I said. "I should think they would."

"Much more than Mrs. Brown gave them—that is, I assume that it was she. The meter is rather—uh—unsteady and there are a number of misspellings and—uh—so on."

"I see." I nodded; and that was one mystery cleared up.

I'd wondered about that, how she could have brought herself to show those "nasty, filthy poems" to anyone. Now I knew.

Poor Ellen. She'd probably slaved all of a couple of hours over the things, her child's face puckered in concentration, lips moving with the scratching of her pencil. She'd show Mister Brownie she wasn't so dumb. Yes, and he wouldn't get a single penny of her imminent riches.

Miss Wakefield wheezed suddenly and coughed with a strangled, rasping sound. Her handkerchief moved quickly to her lips.

"Excuse me, Mr. Brown. This low coastal area—*ahummm*— I—*hmmm*—*aah*—find breathing very difficult. Now, returning to your manuscript—"

"I was about to ask," I said, "whether you'd shown it around any."

"Shown—shown it around?"

"To your editorial staff, say. Or do you do all your own reading?"

"Yes," she said firmly. "Yes, I do all my own reading, Mr. Brown. To be perfectly frank, I have no staff, editorial or otherwise. My business is such that I can handle everything nicely by myself."

I was quite sure that it was, but I was glad to hear her say so. The "vanity" publisher is generally not so much publisher as printing salesman. All he needs to start in business is an office and a printing-house connection.

"No," Miss Wakefield went on, "no one has read the poems but me, Mr. Brown. No one whatsoever. I . . . I — uh — it might be, of course, that I shall want to seek an outside opinion as to their merit, but —"

"Yes?"

"But only in the event I contemplated publishing them on a straight royalty basis as opposed to our co-operative plan. You see my position, Mr. Brown? I naturally couldn't assume the entire financial cost of the enterprise without making reasonably sure of the book's salability."

"You shouldn't do it, anyway, Miss Wakefield," I said. "In all fairness to you, I couldn't let you take such a gamble on an unknown author. Just what would my share of the co-operation come to under your co-operative plan?"

"Well" — she had the grace to blush a little — "that would be governed by, uh, various factors."

"Just for the printing, say. And, of course, your own time and expenses."

"Well . . . two thous — eighteen hundred? Fifteen hundred, Mr. Brown?"

The fifteen hundred was it, apparently. She wasn't going any lower. And while I didn't propose to give her anything, I felt a show of reluctance was in order.

"Isn't that rather high, Miss Wakefield?"

"I don't think so." Her voice had firmed. "I think it is quite reasonable. Under the circumstances.

"The circumstances?"

"The circumstances. I have had the manuscript under study for several months. I have laid tentative plans for its publication and promotion. I have made this trip to Pacific City to see you. In short, Mr. Brown, I have already made a substantial investment in the book."

She nodded righteously, emphasizing the gesture with a phlegmish wheeze. The handkerchief went up and down again, and she went on: "Yes, Mr. Brown, I believe fifteen hundred dollars is extremely reasonable. For that modest sum you retain the undivided rights to the book and all profits accruing therefrom."

"Providing," I said, "there are any."

"Naturally. No publisher can guarantee that a book will be successful. I do believe, however, that this one stands a very good chance, Mr. Brown. I am so strongly of that opinion that I am almost of a mind to publish it on a straight royalty basis, without the customary subsidy. After all, there has been a great deal of publicity about these — *hummm* — so-called Sneering Slayer murders, and a manuscript by the husband of one of the victims —"

"Just a minute," I said. "Let's make a supposition, Miss Wakefield. Let's suppose that I demand the immediate return of that manuscript."

"Do you?"

"Not at all. A mere hypothesis."

"We-ell ... I look on it this way, Mr. Brown. Your name is not on the manuscript, but Mrs. Brown said it was yours and in the absence of any contrary proof—any, uh, dispute—I would feel justified in assuming that you were the author. On the other hand—"

"Yes," I said. "On the other hand, Miss Wakefield?"

"I have an investment in the manuscript, made in good faith. If I should find myself threatened with the loss of that investment—if, that is, you should demand the return of the poems—I think I should insist upon proof that they were yours."

Very neat, no? Despite my personal involvement in the situation, I felt a sneaky admiration for the old girl.

"Do you have the manuscript with you, Miss Wakefield?"

"It is in the hotel safe, Mr. Brown. Manuscripts are such precious things. I live in dread that one may be burned up or lost or—uh—"

"I'd like to go through it with you," I said. "Why don't I pick you up in my car this evening, and we can drive out some place for dinner? I—"

"Please!" The oysters did vigorous sit-ups. "Thank you so much, Mr. Brown, but I'm afraid it would be impossible. I'm not at all a well woman. I require a great deal of rest even after the light sedentary duties of a quiet day. And in the damp— *ahhh-hummm*—night air.... Unthinkable, Mr. Brown. Now, I *could* have the manuscript brought up here, or we might examine it in the lobby."

"It's not important," I said, "and I imagine you'd rather not, wouldn't you? As long as any doubt remains about our future relations?"

"Well, yes, Mr. Brown. I think I would like to have a definite commitment before"—wheeze, cough, and handkerchief— "before turning the manuscript over to you for—uh—study and revision."

"I understand. Now I don't know—it's just possible that I might not be able to do the revisions to my own satisfaction. I might prefer to leave the book unpublished rather than have it be a discredit to me."

"Oh, I'm sure it wouldn't be! I'm confident you can do a wonderful job, Mr. Brown."

"But the other possibility exists, Miss Wakefield. What would be your attitude if it materialized?"

"We-well—" She hesitated quite a bit over that one. "Of course, I already have an investment in the project. My time and—uh—expenses. And, of course, the typesetting and the time on the printing presses must be contracted for in advance…"

Very good again, no? If it was blackmail—and I was by no means sure that it was—it would be very hard to prove.

"I—uh—believe I would have to declare your money forfeit, Mr. Brown. I would be compelled to."

"Naturally. Certainly," I said. "Well…fifteen hundred dollars, eh?"

"I'm sure you can obtain it, Mr. Brown. I—uh—due to the nature of this business, I am forced to inquire into a prospective author's financial situation, and your wife was quite helpful. I understand that you draw a comfortable salary—one which might be borrowed against substantially—and you have a pension and a car and a quantity of furniture. And, doubtless, there are friends who would—"

"Yes," I said, "I think I can probably—How long were you

going to be in town, Miss Wakefield? I suppose you want to conclude the transactions before you leave?"

She said that was exactly what she wanted to do. Travel was expensive and a serious drain on her energies, and there was really nothing to be gained—was there?—by delay. "Today is Monday. I would have to leave here no later than Friday night. I—uh—I wouldn't care to go to greater expense, and I have an appointment with my doctor in Los Angeles on Saturday morning."

"I'm sure I can get it by Friday," I said. "It may be rather late in the day, since I have to work. But—"

"Oh?" She frowned. "I hope it wouldn't be very late. If I don't check out of my room by five, I have to pay for another day."

"I'll keep in touch with you," I said. "If it should happen that I couldn't meet you until after five, you could check out and wait for me in the lobby. Or you could have your dinner here while you're waiting."

"Ye-es, I could do that. But is there a train—?"

"There's one at six-thirty, nine, and eleven-thirty. Of course, you'd be on your way long before eleven-thirty."

I wasn't just woofing, as Stukey would say. Constance Wakefield didn't know it, but she was on her way already.

"Well"—she peered at me carefully, nodded—"that should be all right. Of course, if I could get away sooner—"

"Possibly you can," I said. "I'll do my very best, Miss Wakefield, and possibly I can get you away before Friday."

I promised to keep in touch and went back to the office. At the first opportunity, I dipped into a volume supplied us by the U.S. Weather Bureau. The weather and meteorological conditions in general are must news items in places like Pacific City. I used the volume regularly, and, to the best of my recollection, there would be no moon—

I was wrong. I stared down at the page, weighing the importance, if any, of my error.

Thursday—not Friday—was the moonless night. On Friday there would be a crescent moon. Perhaps, then—? I shook my head, and closed the book.

The light wasn't sufficient to be a factor. It would be dark enough on Friday. Absolute darkness would have been preferable, of course, but Constance might not cooperate on Thursday. She wouldn't be anxious enough. She'd still have a day to spare, and she might decide to use it.

So Friday it would be. I'd send Constance along to her Maker then, and she'd need some repairs when she arrived. It would be a pleasure. There was no alternative—as I saw it.

Perhaps she didn't see the connection between the manuscript poems and the poems found in the possession of Ellen and Deborah. But it was there to be seen, and sooner or later— probably sooner—it would be. Certainly Stukey would spot it. He'd know how to follow it up, expand it into evidence.

Two poems were useless to him. He might back-trail me for years without ever identifying them with a typewriter that I had had access to. Or if he did manage to do so, what of it? Other people had used the same typewriters. They could have written the poems as well as I.

With the manuscript, however, his job would be simplicity itself. He'd have more than fifty poems to work on. He'd turn up one typewriter I'd used after another. He'd follow me back and back, tracing me through the years, checking the typewriters in every place I'd lived or worked. No one else, of course, would have duplicated my trail. They wouldn't have been in all or even a great many of the places I had been in. By sheer weight, if nothing else, the evidence would prove me the author of the Sneering Slayer poems.

It was unfortunate that the author of the poems was so definitely associated with the author of the murders. Unfortunate, that is, for Constance. I'd convinced Lovelace that the two were the same man, and he'd forced Stukey to adopt that theory—at least, Stukey voiced no other in his public pronouncements. And he and we were the chief information sources of the out-of-town newspapers.

The poet was the killer. The point was indisputable—thanks to me. And it was too bad for Constance, but Constance had put herself on the spot. Constance should have stood in Los Angeles.

I called her the following afternoon. I told her I'd been turned down by the bank but that a friend had promised to help, and I'd probably have the money in a day or two.

I let the next day, Wednesday, slide without calling. Around four, on Thursday, I gave her another ring.

The friend would let me have only half the money, and only on condition that I was able to raise the other half. But, I went on, there was absolutely no reason to worry. I knew exactly where I could get the remaining seven hundred and fifty—from an old army pal who would be in town on Friday. Late Friday morning or possibly in the afternoon. He'd been away on vacation and—

She was just a little perturbed. She wheezed and coughed, and said she *did* hope I didn't fail her.

I said I wouldn't.

Friday came. I called her shortly before noon and again at four o'clock. The second call, I told her, was being made from the home of my vacationing friend. He was due to drive up at any moment. As soon as he did, we'd go to the other friend's house and assemble the money. All this would take a little time, of course; they'd probably have to scurry around and get some checks cashed. Perhaps, if she didn't hear from me within the next couple hours, she'd better go on to the station. I'd meet her there with the money—in plenty of time to catch the nine-o'clock train.

Well. She really wheezed and sneezed on that one. This was extremely aggravating, Mr. Brown. All this uncertainty and delay—and sitting around a drafty depot in the night air! Unless I was absolutely sure...

I was sure.

At two minutes of nine, just as she was heading with angry determination toward the Los Angeles train, I had a redcap page her. She hesitated (I was watching her from a bar across the street). Then she trudged after the redcap to the telephone, and I returned to the booth in the bar.

She was boiling angry—wheezing like a teakettle. I cooled her off fast.

I told her I was tired and disgusted myself. I'd been on the move all day, not waiting around for someone else to do something. I'd finally got my two friends together, and they expected to turn up the money within the next couple hours. If that was unsatisfactory to her, all she had to do was say so and—

No, I wasn't going to traipse way down there with part of the money. There was no reason why I should. I'd bring it all when I came — a couple of hours at the outside — but if she didn't care to wait it was perfectly all right with me.

She decided to wait.

I called her at eleven-fifteen.

I simply couldn't make it tonight, I said. There wasn't the slightest doubt about being able to get the money; it wasn't a question of money but time. So, inasmuch as she'd checked out of her hotel and already bought her ticket, I suggested that she go on back to Los Angeles. I'd drive up with the money tomorrow afternoon.

She wheezed and sighed. "Very well, Mr. Brown. I understand that this is a perfectly hideous train, and — But, very well. Tomorrow afternoon, then, without fail."

"Or sooner," I said.

I left the bar and hurried up to the corner of the block. I crossed the intersection and went on across the tracks, pausing at the end of a string of freight cars.

The "milk train" — two freight cars and a mail car, with an antiquated coach hooked on at the rear — was drawn up in front of the station. The engineer and the conductor-brakeman were leaning against a baggage truck, gossiping while they waited for the time to pull out.

Miss Wakefield came out of the station. Weaving with the weight of her suitcase, she had almost reached the coach when the conductor-brakeman saw her. He called, "Hey, lady" — and motioned. She came toward him and he sauntered toward her, letting her do most of the walking. He relieved her of her ticket, shrugged indifferently at some comment or question, and walked back to the engineer.

Miss Wakefield struggled up the steps of the coach and disappeared into the dimly lit interior.

I waited, studying the hands of my watch. Eleven twenty-five, eleven twenty-six, eleven twenty-eight, eleven.... The engineer climbed into his cab. The conductor boosted himself into the mail car and began waving his lantern. It was as I'd been sure it would be. She was the only passenger. The railroad loses—or claims it loses—money on its milk-train passengers and does everything possible to discourage them.

There was a cry of "Bo-o-ard," followed by a crisp *choo-toot!* The train jerked and began to move.

I ran down the line of freight cars, swung crouching into the open vestibule of the coach. I hung there for a few hundred yards, until we were well past the last of the station sheds and platforms. Then I stood up and went inside the car.

Only the lights at each end were burning. She was about midway of the car, sitting with her back toward me and her legs up on another seat. She'd taken her glasses off and laid them on the window sill. As I bent over her, the oysterish eyes blinked in the darkness, staring up at me blankly.

She didn't recognize me. I doubt that she even recognized me as another person. I was only a shadow among shadows—a Something which suddenly shoved her down in the seat and flipped the back rest over on her, pinning her helpless against the worn plush.

She coughed and wheezed. Her mouth dropped open.

I poured a handful of coins into it, and she choked and strangled, rattling them dully.

She'd wanted money. Ellen had wanted to be burned up

and Deborah had wanted—wanted something else—and Constance Wakefield had wanted money. So I'd given it to her, and in such a way as to give her the utmost pleasure from it.

Most people never get a chance to enjoy their money, you know. They strive for it, they get it, and then they are dead. Constance, now—well, Constance would get some satisfaction from hers. It would probably take her an hour or more to strangle. She'd have the money all to herself, with no worries about losing it or someone's taking it away from her.

Possibly she could even take it with her when she died. Part of it, at least. No undertaker would look at her any more than he had to. Any money within her would stand a good chance of remaining there.

Yes, I had done all right by Constance. I had given her money and the opportunity to enjoy it. All that remained now was to relieve her of the manuscript.

It was in her suitcase. I took it out, re-shut the suitcase, and selected a poem at random with handkerchief-covered fingers.

I stuffed the poem into her purse. I gave her a pat on the head and ran back to the vestibule.

The train was still loafing along at approximately twenty miles an hour. I climbed down to the bottom step of the car and dropped off, within a hundred yards of my shack.

Constance Wakefield.... I scrambled up the embankment to my yard, thinking about her.

How could I have done this so calmly, as though it were a relatively unimportant act in a crowded day? Had I actually reached a point where murder meant nothing to me?

The problem disturbed me but only in a remote well-I-should-be-ashamed way. Actually, I could feel no guilt. Ellen, yes. I was honestly sorry about Ellen. And certainly I was something more than sorry about Deborah. But I had entertained no remorse over Constance. She had not been alive, as they had. She would not have gone on living as they would have, except for my intervention. There had been no life in her, only phlegm and avarice, and how can one take life where none is present?

No, I couldn't feel sorry for Constance. I had done the decent thing, put an end to her poor counterfeit of life in the most suitable way possible.

I reached the top of the embankment. I dropped the manuscript into the incinerator and continued on across the yard.

I was very tired. Tired and just a little sick at my stomach. I wanted to get into the house and undress and slug down a few stiff ones.

I'd done the only thing I could do. I'd had to kill her, so, since it had to be done, I'd tried to make the best of it. But still...

"Where have you been?" said Kay Randall. "You answer me, Clinton Brown! *Where have you been?*"

20

I was taken completely by surprise. I didn't know why or how she had come here, and for the moment I was too startled to ask. I could only think of one thing: that I was in a spot and that I'd have to kill her to get out of it.

"Where have you been?" she repeated. "Where is he? What are you up to?"

"Why—why, Kay!" I said. "What do you mean, where is—?"

"You're up to something! You've got him mixed up in it! That's where he's been all these nights when he was supposed to—"

"Kay," I said, "I don't know what you're talking about. I just stepped out in the back yard a few minutes for a breath of air, and—"

"You did not! I've been parked out in the road for almost a half hour, j-just waiting and wondering what to do and—you didn't come out of the house! You've been somewhere! You've—"

"Now, that's nonsense," I said. "Where would I go without my car? It's a dark night, and you just didn't see me when I—"

"You're lying!" She shrieked it out. "You haven't been in the back yard. Y-You—I don't know what you're up to, but I'll find out! You'll see! You're not going to get away with—"

I'd been edging toward her, and she'd been backing away,

and now we were at the side of the house. I reached for her, and she struck at me. Wildly, hysterically. She screamed again that I was lying and that she intended to find out why.

"You'll see! You can't mix Dave up in your dirty—"

The door of the house opened abruptly. Tom Judge peered out.

"Hey, Brownie," he said. "Haven't you had enough air yet? Your drink's getting all warm."

I didn't know what he was doing here either, but obviously he hadn't come with Kay. It appeared, rather, that he had heard her accusations—as anyone within a hundred yards would have—and was lending me his support.

"I'll be right with you," I said, more or less automatically. "Fix me another drink, huh?"

"Sure," he said, giving Kay a superbly insolent stare. "Be careful you don't catch cold—or something."

He slammed the door on that, so hard that her head rocked back. She turned slowly back to me, lifted and dropped her hands helplessly.

"I—I'm sorry," she said. "I've j-just been so worried, and—and frightened. I kn-know there must be a good reason why he's lied to me, b-but—"

"Why haven't you asked him?" I said. "You indicated that he's been misrepresenting his whereabouts at night for some time."

"I—well, I—"

"That would be a little too direct, wouldn't it? A little too straightforward and honest? You'd rather sneak around and raise hell with—"

"Well!" She flared up. "You *are* trying to get him into trouble,

aren't you? You're mean and rotten and hateful, and you're trying to make him the same way!"

"Well," I said, "at least I haven't tried to poison him."

She gave me a puzzled look, then turned and took a step
toward the road. "Clint"—she hesitated—"I'm sorry. Don't
pay any attention to me, hmmm?"

"You can depend on it," I said. "Now and upon all other
occasions."

"And—a-and please don't tell Dave I was here."

"Why not?" I said. "The wife of my best friend visits me late
at night. Why shouldn't I, as an honorable and upright man,
inform him of the fact?"

"Please, Clint. I'm—I'm a-afraid. He isn't himself any more....
Like tonight, now. I'd checked with the Civic League and I
knew there wasn't any meeting, so—"

So she'd told him he was going to stay at home. Oh, she
didn't call him a liar or anything like that. She'd been very
sweet and tactful about the matter. Father had simply been killing himself with work, and she was going to put a stop to it.
Meeting or no meeting, Father was going to go to bed and get a
good night's rest. And, then, playfully but firmly, she'd taken
his car keys.

"He wouldn't talk to me, Clint. He just sat and stared, looking at me something—something awful! I went back to the
bedroom for a minute, and when I came out he was gone. I
guess he must have slipped out and hailed a taxicab."

"Well—" I said.

"Of course, I'm not sure he didn't have to go to some of those
other meetings. But if he lied about this one—"

"I see," I said. "Very interesting."

I could have named her two nights when Dave had attended nonexistent meetings, but I could see nothing to be gained by it. I had a hunch that the affair was one to proceed on with great caution.

"Clint. What do you s-suppose—?"

"I don't," I said. "There's probably some very simple explanation for the whole thing, Kay. One that will doubtless surprise you with its simplicity when it finally dawns on you."

"Well"—she shrugged tiredly—"I hope so. I'll—I suppose I better go on back home. Good night, Clint."

"Are you going to ask Dave where he's been? When he shows up, that is?"

"N-No," she said, and it seemed to me that she shivered. "I—I don't think I'd better. I'd rather not know if—if—Good night, Clint."

"Good night," I said.

I walked with her to the road and watched as she got into the car and drove off. Then I went into the house.

Tom had a drink waiting for me. Judging by his appearance, I suspected that he had several in his stomach in addition to the one in his hand.

"Hope you don't mind my busting in on you this way," he said, his chin jutting with a trace of belligerence. "Your car was here, and I figured you must be around. Thought you'd just gone for a little walk or something."

"Quite all right," I said. "I hope I didn't keep you waiting long?"

"Huh-uh." He dumped more whisky into his glass. "Don't think it was—couldn't have been more than a few minutes. Seems like I'd just got here when I heard Miss Beauty Bitch yelling at you."

I nodded. Time does indeed fly by when one is stowing away free drinks.

"Boy," he went on, "would I like to give that bitch a good sock in the mush! She was at the Christmas party last year, y'know, the one all the wives came to. Playing up to Lovelace and his old lady, and giving everyone else the snoot. Midge— well, Midge was wearing a dress she'd made over and I thought it looked pretty nice, but Miss Bitch poked fun at it all evening. You know, pretending like she admired it and asking how much it had cost new, and so on, and all the time laughing about it. Boy, I could have murdered her!"

I said that Kay was like the weather: everyone talked about her but no one did anything. He scowled surlily, rocking the ice in his glass.

"She screws around with me, there'll be something done," he promised. "And that goes for Dave, too. Y'know, I always kind of liked the guy, Brownie. You know I did. An' then he turns around and sics that goddamned Stukey on me. Gets me arrested for murder."

"I didn't know that," I said. And I hadn't known—only suspected—that Randall had phoned in the tip to Stukey. "I supposed that the cab driver had—"

"Huh-uh. They didn't have any driver in to identify me like they would have, so I figured it had to be someone else. And the way I figured, it couldn't have been anyone but Dave. We were the only ones in the office at the time she called, see? Maybe he didn't know it was her, but he knew about what time she got into town and he saw me taking a straight-line call over your phone. And that was enough for him. Oh, he did it, all right. I was going to let it slide, but after I heard about this job in L.A. I decided to tell him off before I left town. The bastard admitted he'd done it. Said he hadn't meant to be underhanded; just hadn't felt free to give his name to the cops because the paper was involved."

I shook my head sympathetically. "I'm sure he didn't think you were really guilty," I said. "Dave's just overly conscientious. He saw you take the call and—"

"So what? I saw him take some, too, but I didn't go running to the cops about it. We were alone in the office. He could have talked to her through the desk phone. I'm not saying he did, understand. Just that he could have. If I'd wanted to be a bastard, I could've got him in a jam like he did me."

"Yes," I said. "Very forbearing of you.... But what's this about Los Angeles?"

"I'm pulling out, me and the family. We've sold our furniture, and we're heading for L.A. in the morning. I—Oh, yeah. Let me give you this before I forget."

He pulled a roll of bills from his pocket and flipped me a twenty. I hesitated, wanting to give it back to him, then nodded and thanked him. He was very much on edge, more resentfully watchful than usual. He might consider the gift of the twenty an insult.

"You said you had a job in Los Angeles? What paper?"

"Well—uh—it's not definite. They want a top rewrite man, see, and I said I was entirely willing to come in and show 'em what I could do, so—well, I can handle it, all right. They tell me it's actually a hell of a lot easier to work on those big-city dailies. They've got plenty of help, you know. They don't expect you to knock yourself out like you have to on the *Courier*."

I wanted to say, *You won't last a shift, boy. There'll be a deadline every hour, and all hell will pop if you miss one. There's no time to work your stuff over. You have to hit it on the nose the first shot. And you can't let everything else slide while you're doing it. You'll have to keep answering your phones, two of them, taking down notes on other stories. You'll have a half dozen stories going at the same time. Sure, they've got plenty of help; they need it. And whether you knock yourself out or not is up to you. That's strictly your own problem, and they're not concerned with it. You...*

But why tell him something that he probably already knew? The truth, which fear and false pride kept him from admitting?

"Tom," I said, "that's swell. I know you'll make out fine, boy."

"Yeah," he said, frowning down vaguely at the floor. "I've got to, so I guess I will. I—I've got to get out of this burg. I can't... There's nothing around here for me."

He took another outsize drink, gulped it, shuddered, and stood up. "Well, I guess I better shove off. Guess I ought to have gone home long ago. I've been out wandering around since about six, kind of giving the old town a last once-over, and Midge might be getting worried."

I offered to drive him home, but he declined. He'd just take a taxi, he guessed. He'd just remembered that there was a fellow in town he wanted to see, and...

I called a cab for him. We shook hands and he left.

I had an idea that I was acquainted with the fellow he wanted to see, that one and all the other bartenders in town. And I could understand his unease and restlessness. He couldn't have got more than a couple of hundred bucks for his furniture. With that and a wife and baby—and almost no ability—he was tackling one of the toughest towns and toughest jobs in the world.

What would he do when his money ran out? What does a man do when he can accept nothing less than the unachievable?

It was difficult to say, I thought. There was no telling what Tom Judge would do. Something desperate, of course, something foolish. But exactly what...?

21

Subconsciously, I think I must have been prepared for an unusual aftermath to my strangling of Constance Wakefield. I must have been — for I was not particularly startled when that aftermath came — and it seems only logical that I should have been so prepared. This was my third murder, the third time I had gone through the motions of murder. Yet in each of the first two cases...

I couldn't be positive that I'd killed Ellen. I'd slugged her and set fire to her, but she hadn't died of the blow or the flames. Asphyxiation had been the cause of death, and it did seem strange that, once on her feet, she couldn't have escaped from that small cabin.

I couldn't be positive that I'd killed Deborah. I'd left her alone in the shack and she'd been lying so very still when I returned. And in my haste to get the hateful deed over — Well? How could I be sure? How could I know that she wasn't already dead when I broke her neck?

So with Constance Wakefield — my "murder" number three. Murder in quotes, yes, for here again there was a strong element of doubt. Again I couldn't be sure that I had actually killed. In fact, it seemed quite certain that I hadn't.

Her body was found late the following morning. It was lying beside the railroad tracks about thirty miles outside of Pacific City.

There was a handful of dimes in her purse and, of course, the poem.

Her death was attributed to heart failure, with concussion a contributory factor.

It was believed that she had fallen or been pushed from the train, with the emphasis very heavily on the *fallen*.

After all, there'd been no other passengers in the coach — the train crew swore to that. And the train hadn't stopped until it was almost seventy miles up the line. True, there was the poem, but that had been penciled over and marked up so much as to be almost indecipherable. It could not be definitely stated that it was another of the Sneering Slayer rhymes. There was at least as good a chance that, intrigued by the other poems, she had tried her hand at one herself.

She was a publisher, wasn't she? She'd be interested in such things, wouldn't she?

Of course, the police were "investigating thoroughly" and "leaving no stone unturned" but what they expected to find under those stones was obviously nothing.

The old girl was half blind. The coach was dark. She'd gone out to the rear platform for some fresh air — a rarity on the milk train — and taken a tumble.

Yes, I am aware of the holes in this line of reasoning. But since this is fact, not fiction, there is nothing I can do about them. If they irritate you sufficiently, you might take them up with the police of the next county, where Miss Wakefield's body was discovered.

I wouldn't say they were stupid. I am reasonably confident, say, that they are capable of tracking an elephant through a snow drift. They could do it, but they wouldn't — unless the elephant was traveling more than thirty miles an hour or sneaking fruit from the orange groves. They would see no occasion to. It would be a "needless expense." And the cops in the next county, like the cops in so many other counties, are under firm edict not to waste the taxpayers' money.

So that was the way things stood with Constance Wakefield. The cops *believed* it was an accident. They finished their thorough investigation with its incidental upturning of stones in some forty-eight hours, and they were *convinced* it was an accident.

The Los Angeles papers tried to build the case up as murder. They whooped it up, mixing its meager facts in with rewrites of the previous two cases. And they even sent their own "special investigators" into the county. That went on for three or four days, and then there was a nice juicy murder right in Los Angeles — a B-girl carved up and hidden in, of all places, an ice cream cart — and you can guess what happened to the Wakefield story. To hell with that. *This* was something hot.

Although I had seen evidence of great shrewdness in Lem Stukey, I was still surprised at his positive conviction that Constance Wakefield had been murdered. Or, I should say, I was surprised at the insight that brought him to that conviction.

"Maybe I wouldn't feel that way if she'd died in this county." He grinned. "I'd probably let it slide just like those guys are doing. But I figure they got to see it, even if they ain't doing anything about it. Look, now, just looky here. The first one he sets on fire. The next one he tosses to the dogs. The third one he pushes off a train. He —"

"Hold it," I said. "How did he know it was going to kill her when he pushed her off the train?"

"You ain't listening, keed. You're stealing my stanzas. He don't know it's going to kill her. That's what I'm talking about. He couldn't be sure, and he couldn't be sure that what he did to Ellen was going to finish her, and this Mrs. Chasen — he couldn't be—"

"Hold it again," I said. "He could have finished her off before he put her in the—"

"I tell you it's a pattern," Stukey insisted. "I can't lay it out for you like wallpaper, but it's got to be the same guy. He don't carry through, see? He leaves too much to chance. He ain't— well, he don't seem serious about it."

"Murder isn't serious?"

"So maybe he don't really mean to murder 'em. He thinks he does, maybe, but all he's really up to is a rough sort of kidding. You watch a bunch of youngsters sometime, keed. They'll start off talking, razzing each other, and pretty soon they've used up all the dirty cracks they got and they start punching. They're fed up with the talk, see, so they start making with the fists. . . . It figures, pal. You really want to kill someone, you don't play around at it like this guy. You get you a knife or a gun, and you do the job fast and permanent."

I found myself staring at him. I wondered if . . .

". . . Take them dimes in her purse now." He was talking about Constance again. "There was thirty-three of them, wasn't there? And what would a dame be doin' with more than two or three dimes in her purse? I'd say that that was all she did have, Brownie. The guy that bumped her put the other thirty there. He was razzing her, see? Thirty pieces of silver, like Judas got paid off with."

I lighted a cigarette. I said I would like to offer him my theory.

"I'm convinced," I said, "that she was killed by an enraged red-cap. Driven mad by dime tips, he followed her onto the train and poured the dimes down her throat with the intent to strangle her. Then, driven by the wild strength born of fear, she disgorged the dimes—frugally stowing them away in her purse—and—"

"Yeah?" He waited a moment for me to continue, then shrugged. "So go on and laugh about it. For all you know he maybe did exactly that. Not any redcap, dammit. The guy that did the other two jobs would fit his pattern."

I asked him how some of his other theories fitted into the pattern, as, for example, his one-time belief that Tom Judge had killed Ellen.

"You say that the same man killed all three. But he was in jail at the time Mrs. Chasen was killed, and he was with me on the night of Miss Wakefield's demise."

"Yeah, I know." He frowned doggedly. "So I can't lay it all out for you. I don't know all the answers. All I'm saying is that every killing's got the same earmarks, and it ain't got 'em accidentally. The same guy's mixed up in—in—"

"Yes?"

"Nothing. What the hell? I was just going to say that it looks almost like two guys. One of 'em, this joker, he half-asses the job up and the second one makes it stick. Now, wait a minute!" He held up a hand. "I said it *looked* that way. I didn't say it was that way."

"You know," I said, "that's a very interesting idea, Stuke. Why don't you work on it?"

"Me? Now that the guy's finally pulled out of the county?"

He shook his head firmly. "Not me, keed. He ain't no skin off my nose from now on."

The *Courier* carried the Wakefield story one day and gave it a back-page squib in one edition the next. And that was the last Pacific City residents heard of her, unless they read the out-of-town papers.

Mr. Lovelace felt that the story lacked local interest. He felt that it was "negative"— the sort of news we'd been printing far too much of lately. We'd have to have less of it from now on, much, much less. It was "unconstructive." It was "depressing." It took up space needed for "worthwhile" items.

He was very firm during our discussion, and I made no very large effort to soften him up. The clean-up campaign *was* getting a little tiresome. At least, I was getting very tired of writing about it. It was the same thing day after day, dry, repetitious— completely lacking in any possibilities for humor. And with the murderer supposedly gone from Pacific City, the basis for keeping it alive was gone.

So I didn't argue with Lovelace at any length or with any great insistence. Perhaps you "couldn't legislate public morals." Perhaps "these things worked themselves out if you gave them time." And perhaps I knew damned well that it would do me no good to argue.

There was that in his manner which said as much.

The discussion was embarrassing to him, for some reason. He seemed prepared to be angry if forced to continue it.

All things considered, it seemed a poor time to test my influence with him.

The clean-up story had been getting a daily play in every edition. We dropped it to one edition a day, then to one every other day, then one every three days. And very soon we had dropped it completely.

There was no further mention of it after that. No further mention of the murders. The paper resumed its puerile emptiness, a newspaper in name only as I was a man in name only. There was nothing in either of us. We were façades for emptiness.

Broadly speaking, things became as they were before the murders. Yet the outlines of those things were becoming dimmer to me. It was hard to reach out to them any more — lash out at them any more. It was difficult to remember why I had ever wanted to.

Dave Randall was as he had always been. A little more nervous and jumpy, perhaps, but generally unchanged. So, likewise, with Lovelace and Stukey and everyone else. All the same, as I was the same. And still a change had taken place.

They were receding from me, growing hazier and wobblier of outline. It was increasingly hard to bring them back into focus.

I wondered if the booze could be responsible, and I swore off for twelve of the longest hours in my existence. It was not enough, of course; months would be required to desaturate me. But further abstinence was unthinkable. Perhaps I could not go on as I had without serious consequences, but neither could I stop. It made me too ill physically. The clarity it brought me was not the kind I desired.

Without whisky, that circle in my mind began to dissolve, I ceased to move around it endlessly, and my vision turned inward. And while I caught only a glimpse of what lay there, that little was so bewildering and maddening — and frightful — that I could look no more.

I tried cutting down gradually on the whisky, and I have continued to try. But these attempts like the other have not been successful. When I reach a certain stage in the cutting down, the circle begins to dissolve, and I must quickly reverse the cutting-down process. I —

I am not like that; that which I caught a glimpse of is not me. I will not accept it nor look at it.

But I am getting ahead of myself again. I am rushing toward the end, and the end will come soon enough.

The emptiness, the meaninglessness went on. Pushing the others farther away from me. Pushing them out of my reach.

It was unbearable. I could not let them go. They were the life I did not have, my one handhold on existence. I had to do something. And I did.

We have a Republican postmaster in Pacific City, and he owes a considerable political debt to the *Courier*. He was glad to let me look into the records of money orders issued. I went back through them. I found what I was looking for within an hour.

Except that I had some idle time to pass, I had no reason to look farther. Nevertheless, I did look, and what I found was definitely not what I had expected to find.

I was puzzled, startled, at first. Then the puzzledness gave way to excitement, and a curious kind of relief.

So this was it. This was why, and possibly how...

Well, it was the day before yesterday when I made the discovery; and as I entered the house the phone rang. It was Stukey. He was up on the Hill, he said, up in Italian town. He'd been kind of takin' it easy this afternoon—just sorta screwing around and cutting up touches with the boys. If I wasn't doing nothing, maybe he'd pick up some grub and saunter on down to the shack.

I said that would be fine, I'd been hoping he would call. He said, swell, he'd be right down then. He was on foot, yeah; he'd sent his car back to the station. But it was a nice day, and he kind of felt like walkin' and...

"Fine," I said. "That's perfect, Stuke."

22

He brought steaks, et cetera, and prepared them as before.

We ate as we had before, myself at the coffee table, he from a tray placed upon a chair.

We finished eating and I reached for the whisky bottle. He tilted his chair back against the wall, sipping a bottle of the beer he had brought.

He was giving the beer a play for a while, he said. He'd been hittin' the old whiz too hard, and a guy could only do that so long before it got him. It sneaked up on him before he knew it. Maybe it didn't show on him, but—well, what was the sense in waitin' until you was knocked out? Ain't that the way you see it, keed?

I shook my head. Nodded. Shrugged. I wasn't thinking about what he was saying. I was wondering how I could bring the subject up, how to best mention my discovery.

It should be done obliquely, I thought. I should come in at an angle, letting him see the approach but leaving its terminus in temporary doubt. First a small hint, then a stronger one—watching him, smiling at him. Turning the heat on gradually and—

And letting him sweat.

He rambled on aimlessly, pausing now and then for some

comment from me. I nodded and shrugged and shook my head, and finally he lapsed into silence.

That lasted for several minutes, or what I believe on reflection was several minutes. Then he let the legs of his chair down to the floor and announced that maybe he'd better go. I looked kind of tired, like I didn't feel too good, so—

I came out of my reverie. I said that I wouldn't think of letting him go. "We haven't been seeing nearly enough of each other," I said. "Tell me, what great deeds are afoot with Pacific City's finest? How goes the fearless pursuit of panhandlers and unlicensed peddlers?"

"Aaaah." He raised and dropped his shoulders uncomfortably. "Lookit here, keed. You're talkin' to the wrong boy about that. You really want to do somethin' about it, which I don't figure you do, I'll tell you who to see."

"Yes?"

"Yeah. You talk to the merchants' association, see how they feel about peddlers. You see how the tourist bureau an' the chamber of commerce feels about panhandlers. They'll say I'm too easy on 'em, keed. I don't treat 'em rough enough."

"But you can't be swayed by outside influences," I said. "I am confident of it. The clean-up campaign is a case in point. . . . You are proceeding with it, are you not? The mere absence of publicity has not deterred you?"

"No," he said, "it ain't."

"I was sure of it. I knew that with one such as you there—"

"Listen to me, keed. I want to tell you somethin'."

I tilted the whisky bottle again. I raised my glass and gestured. "By all means," I said. "You tell me something, and then perhaps I shall tell you something."

"The clean-up's over an' done with, and I ain't sorry. But there ain't a damned thing I could do if I was.... You really don't see it, Brownie? I didn't expect old Lovey to know straight up, but I didn't figure I'd have to draw a map for you. Who do you think owns all these whorehouses and policy joints? Who do you think owns the horse parlors and deadfalls and mitt mills? Well, it ain't the grifters, keed. They just work 'em. And they pay goddamned fancy rents for the privilege. And the people that get them rents swing plenty of weight around town. Sure, I graft. Why not? If the dirty money ain't too dirty for our best people, like they call them, it's plenty clean for me. But I tell you this, pal. If the stuff wasn't there, I couldn't take it."

I looked down at my glass, slowly added more whisky. I shook my head firmly. "That's an old story, Stuke. Every crooked cop I've ever talked to has the same alibi. He'd like to go straight, but—"

"I ain't said I'd like to. I ain't no hero. I'm just telling you why it's this way, and why it's going to keep on being this way. Yeah, it's an old story, all right, but I don't figure you know it very well so I'll give you the rest. There's the fines we take in from those places. We pull the grifters in once a week, they pay their fines, an' then we let 'em go back to work. It's like taxes, keed, and it comes to enough to pay the overhead for the whole damned department. More than a hundred grand a year that them best people—the regular taxpayers—can keep in their pockets. And that's—"

"Stuke. Please," I said. "You don't have to defend yourself to me. I know your conscience is spotless, your soul pure as driven snow, and—"

"You asked for it," he said stubbornly. "I'm telling you. You

claim I'm always layin' into the colored folks—blaming everything that happens on them. Well, maybe I do, kind of, but I
got a damned good reason to. Not one out of a hundred can get
a decent job, a job where he can get as much as you do, say, or
even half as much. They don't make no dough, but they got to
keep laying it on the line. They get stuck every time they turn
around. Their rents cost 'em plenty, because there's just one section of town they can live in. If they don't want to walk two–
three miles to a store in a white neighborhood—where they'll
probably get a good hard snooting—they have to buy from the
little joints in their own section, places where there ain't much
of a selection and the prices are high. It takes every nickel they
can get just to keep goin', just to live like a bunch of animals.
They're always about half sore, an' it don't take much to make
'em more than half. They make trouble; they start playin' rough.
And all me and my boys can do is play a little rougher. Flatten
'em out or get 'em sent up for a stretch. We can't get to the bottom of the trouble, try to fix it so there won't be any more. All
we can do is…All right," Stukey sighed, "go on and laugh at
me. But just the same, I'm giving it to you straight."

"I wasn't laughing at the remarks," I said, "only at their
author. I was wondering what irresistible sociological forces
moved you to offer to hush up a murder that you thought I had
committed, providing I would play ball?"

He hesitated, frowning. I really think he had forgotten all
about it. "All right," he said. "I play along. I got just so much to
work with, and I try to get all I can out of it. What about you?"

"About me?"

"Sure. You're smart. You got a good education and a good

trade. If things don't go to suit you, you can move on to another job. You don't have to play with anyone."

"I don't understand you," I said.

"Why don't *you* do something? You've got influence with Lovelace. You can swing your weight with him, and if he swings back you ain't really lost anything. Me, I'm nothin' to him. If he gets sore at me, I'm sunk. So how's about it, keed? If you really want somethin' done about Pacific City, why don't you go to work on it?"

"It seems to me," I said, "that I've already——"

"Huh-uh. You ain't done nothin', and you ain't goin' to. This clean-up wasn't nothin' to you but a way to swing the old needle. You could make Lovelace squirm. You could turn the heat on me. You could shake everything to hell up, and it gave you a bang. That's all it meant to you. That's all anything means to you. Just a chance to make someone sweat. From what I hear, you've driven this Randall guy halfway off his rocker. You've got him sweatin' blood, afraid he's going to lose his job. But I could tell him he ain't going to lose it. You won't carry things that far; you don't want him to get away from you."

I poured another drink, and for some reason my hand shook.

"Anything else?" I said.

"Uh-huh. The county judge thing is out. I've been studyin' it over, an' I can see it was just a pipe dream. Maybe I could make it, but I wouldn't last much longer than it would take me to open my mouth. That's the way you figured, huh, keed? That's why you wouldn't give me a boost? You knew I'd lose out all the way around, and you couldn't ride me any more."

"That's all?" I said. "You've nothing more to say?"

"I guess that's about it, Brownie." He shrugged good-naturedly. "No hard feelings?"

"I'd like to say something, then. About Ellen. Now, I believe the evidence indicated that she revived after the murderer's attack. She was up on her feet in an enclosure less than fifteen feet square, and yet she couldn't make it to the door or a window. She died of asphyxiation."

"Yeah," Stukey nodded. "Like I was sayin', keed, the guy acted like—"

"I know. Like he wasn't serious. Like he must have had some help from a second guy. Someone, say, who was being black-mailed by her."

He stared at me silently. There was a peculiar hardness in his small round eyes.

"Which raises this question, Stuke," I said. "Why did you send her almost three thousand dollars in a little more than two years' time?"

23

His face went completely blank. Then, slowly, a strange look spread over it—not of fear, as I had expected, but rather a compound of regret and annoyance and, mayhap, embarrassment.

He stood up and went out into the kitchen. I heard the ice box door open and close.

He came back and sat down, a freshly opened bottle of beer in his hand.

"A blackmailer," he said thoughtfully. "Not just a one-shot, not just a gal squeezing a little dough when she was in a pinch, but a steady worker. That's the way you saw your wife, Brownie?"

"I—" I paused. "I asked you a question, Stuke."

"And you got an answer. An' here's one to the next question. Why does a guy give a woman dough? Why would he keep sendin' it to her month after month when he ain't even seein' her?"

I heard a laugh. One that was not mine, although it came from me. "Oh, *no,*" I said. "No, Stuke. That I can't believe."

"I know you can't. I knew you wouldn't. But that don't change nothin'. I liked her—just liked to talk and visit with her, and she seemed to like it, too. She never asked me for no dough; she never tried to make me for a penny. So . . . so maybe that was part of it. Maybe that meant a lot to a guy who never saw a dame without her hand out. I liked her, and when you like someone you try to help 'em."

I laughed again, the laugh that was not my laugh. So he just liked to talk to her, visit with her; *he* was content with that. And I—

Somehow—I believed him.

"That was all, keed. I can buy the other for a hell of a lot less than three grand, and I can get it a lot handier. I don't have to cover up and sneak around. That wasn't easy for me to do, Brownie. Talkin' about her like I did, pretendin' like I thought—"

"Why did you?"

"Why?" He shot me a puzzled glance. "You mean I should show how I felt in front of you? I shouldn't cover up about a guy's own wife? I guess you and me went to different schools, keed."

I reached for my drink, and the glass slipped from my fingers. It bounced from the coffee table and rolled splashing to the floor. I picked up the bottle and drank from it.

"I believe you threatened me," I said. "I was to lay off of this deal or you'd make me wish I had."

"Let's skip it, huh, pal? I wouldn't do it even if you was to try to make somethin' out of this. Maybe it would give you some trouble, but it would hurt me more. If it got around that I was spreadin' a story like—like—"

"Go on," I said.

"Ah, hell, Brownie." He tilted his chair back against the wall. "I was just sore. It—it ain't really nothin'. It didn't make no difference with me, did it? Why, Jesus, I had it doped out right from the beginning almost: that pension, with nothin' wrong showin' on you, an' breaking up with your wife when there wasn't another babe, an' your drinkin' and ridin' everyone, an'—and this place. You wantin' a home—not just a room—and doing your best to have one. It wasn't hard to figure out for a guy that was really interested. So I did, and what the hell? If it didn't mean nothin' to a lowdown jerk like me, why would—"

"You've known all along," I said. "You've let me think—You let me go ahead and—"

He mumbled apologetically. He raised the beer bottle and drank, his head thrown back to avoid my eyes.

He'd let me go ahead and...

It had all started because I was afraid that he...

"Let's talk about somethin' else, huh, keed?" He gave me a pleading look. "About this doll, now, that your friend Randall's been playin'. She's no good in trumps, an' you can tell him I said so. He'd better pull out while he's still able to."

"Doll?" I said. "Doll?"

It didn't register on me. There was no room for it in my mind.

"You didn't know about her? Well, damned near everyone else seems to. The guy's practically been livin' with her at night, and she's the kind that talks." He started to raise the beer bottle again, paused. "Come to think of it, maybe you better not tell him nothin'. Just leave her to me. I'll run the little bitch out of town."

The bottle went up. He threw his head back to receive the beer. Then...

I doubt if he knew what happened then.

I hurled the whisky bottle and it crashed sickeningly against the bottle he was holding. His tilted chair shot from under him. He went over backward in a tinkling shower of glass, and his head hit the floor with a thud.

229

He lay there crumpled and groaning, his face bleeding from a dozen cuts.

I got a length of clothesline rope from the kitchen, swung an end over one of the living-room rafters, and gave him a boost. After all, he'd always wanted me to boost him, hadn't he?

And then I fled the place. I took a room at a hotel. And I have not been back since. And now I am back at the newspaper. The others have all gone, but I think someone has come in, has been sitting in the darkness at the other side of the room. . . .

Of course, I didn't kill him. I know now that I am incapable of killing anyone. He has been missing for more than a day, but not because he is dead. I don't know what — why —

I don't as yet have the answer to certain other questions, I only know that I have not killed and cannot kill, and . . .

He is stirring at last, the man who has been sitting there behind me. He has come forward and his hand has dropped down on my shoulder. It is a well-manicured hand. I can smell the odor of hair oil and talcum powder and freshly shined shoes. The hand moves from my shoulder to the stack of manuscript. It rakes it off the desk and into the wastebasket.

"Jesus, keed. You hadn't ought to write things like that. People might think you're crazy."

24

He grinned down at me through slightly puffed lips. There was a wide strip of adhesive tape across his nose. His talcumed face was a network of red scratches and cuts.

"I look like hell, huh, keed? Jesus, what'd you run out on me for? That wasn't no way to treat a pal. A guy's chair slips out from under him, and he smashes his face on a bottle an'—"

"What—what are you trying to pull?" I said. "You know I tried to kill you. I botched the job the first time, and you've been waiting for me to try again. You've had the shack staked out. You had them give out the report that you were missing, and—"

"Why, keed"—he widened his eyes in exaggerated amazement—"I don't dig you, a-tall. Like I said, my chair slipped. I'd swear to it, Brownie, get me? I'd *swear* it happened that way."

I got him, all right. I was beginning to get him.

I saw what he intended to do, and a shiver of sickness ran through me. "Why?" I said. "Why did you drop the stake-out? What made you see that I wasn't—that I couldn't—"

His grin widened. His eyes shifted a little, and he jerked his head toward the Teletypes. "Looks like you got a lot of news there, keed."

"Why?" I repeated.

"Maybe you ought to take a look: Maybe it's the same news we got at the station a couple hours ago."

I turned slowly. I walked over to the Teletypes. A long streamer of yellow paper drooped from each. I picked up the one from the A.P. machine.

And I read:

LOS ANG IOI AM SPL TO COURIER THOMAS J. JUDGE, UNTIL RECENTLY A REWRITE MAN ON THE PACIFIC CITY COURIER, CONFESSED TODAY TO THE MYSTERIOUS MURDER OF ELLEN TANNER BROWN, ESTRANGED WIFE OF ANOTHER COURIER EMPLOYEE. BROKE AND OUT OF WORK, THE SULLEN STOCKY NEWSMAN TOLD POLICE THAT HE 'JUST WANTED TO GET EVERYTHING OVER WITH.' 'I'M NOT SORRY ABOUT HER,' HE DECLARED. 'SHE HAD IT COMING TO HER.' JUDGE'S EARLY MORNING CONFESSION TO LOS ANGELES AUTHORITIES EXPLODED A WIDELY HELD THEORY THAT MRS. BROWN'S DEATH WAS ONE OF THREE SOCALLED SNEERING SLAYER MURDERS. WHILE UNABLE TO EXPLAIN CERTAIN SIMILARITIES
MORE MORE MORE

I swallowed heavily, and my head swam for a moment. Then I read on down the yellow stream into the additional dispatches.

Tom had been lying under the cottages (while I was there) and had returned to consciousness from his drunken stupor (just after I left). He was miserable and thoroughly angry. He had been sorely mistreated, as he saw it; she had lured him there and then laughed at him.

He crawled out from beneath one of the cottages and re-entered hers. She, half hysterical and painfully burned — and engaged in trying to beat out the fire in the bed — had hurled herself at him. He had brutally knocked her to the floor. Then, frightened by what he had done, he had hastily wiped up the room with his coat and fled. There was no actual intent to kill, of course, but still he *had* brought about her death. He had — and I hadn't. And I knew it was the truth.

"Well, Brownie?" Stukey said. "I guess that cleans it up, don't it?"

I stared at him blankly, thinking about Tom Judge, thinking of how much alike Tom and I were. Doubtless that was why I had always detested him so much, because he was so accurate a mirror of my own faults. Tom demanded the benefit of all doubts, but he could give no one the benefit of any. A frown was suspicious, but so also was a smile. . . . Tom Judge, plowing stubbornly down one rocky path when he could have moved over into an easier and friendlier one. He wouldn't try to reorient himself. He wouldn't try to adapt himself to another way of life which, while it would not have been wholly satisfactory, could have been far better than the one he had. Not Tom. Not me. We preferred being miserable, martyring ourselves. Living not as men but human gadflies.

"You see, keed? I figured like everyone else that the three deaths were all tied together. That's what had me thrown. But when this Judge character confessed, I seen right away that you hadn't —"

Stukey had been right about me. I hadn't wanted any change.

All I had wanted was to keep everyone under my thumb, to gouge and nibble away at them while I watched them squirm.... Dave Randall. He hadn't always let Kay wear the pants in the family. It was I, not Kay, who had stripped him of all his self-confidence. She had merely taken over where I left off....So that was the way it was. Then, when I wearied of the game, when I could no longer continue it, I would kill myself. Or, no—No! I would make *Them* kill *me*. I would do something so blatantly criminal—so botched—that They would know I was guilty, and They would have to...

They *would* have to, wouldn't They?

They couldn't leave me to go on...into nothingness.

Stukey was watching me, narrow-eyed. He said, "Get it through your noggin, keed. You—"

"You're wrong," I said. "Tom's lying. I went over to the island that night. We argued, and she threatened me, and—and—"

"Huh-uh." He wagged his head. "He ain't lying. Anyway, you couldn't have been over on the island that night. You couldn't have got across the bay. Everyone knows that."

"I tell you I did! I hit her with the bottle. I—"

"Yeah? How you goin' to prove it—and what if you did? You want to be sent up for a couple of years on an assault charge, Brownie? You want to lay around in a cell with no booze and nothin' to do but think?"

He chuckled softly. But his round little eyes were like brown chunks of ice.

"I killed Mrs. Chasen," I said. "I met her in Los Angeles when I went up for the funeral, and—"

"You didn't kill her. She killed herself."

"I tell you I *did* kill her!" My voice rose. "I can tell you just how I did it. I'd been out drinking, and when I came back she was lying on the bed asleep and..."

I told him.

He listened thoughtfully, but his head wagged again. "So that was how—" He hesitated. "But you didn't kill her, keed. She was already dead."

"I tell you... What makes you think—?"

"You remember them sleeping pills she had? Five-grain amy-tals? Well, we checked back on the prescription and she'd had it filled the day before. She'd got thirty of those goofballs and there was only five left in her purse."

"But that doesn't prove she took—"

"I'm tellin' you, keed. We didn't have much in the way of a body to work on, but there was plenty of blood. And that blood was loaded with the goofer dust. More than enough to kill her. Sure, I kept it quiet. The deal was futzed up enough as it was, and it didn't make sense. How in the hell if she'd killed herself could she have wound up in the dog pound? I figured maybe the coroner had called his shots wrong. But—well, it makes sense now. She was already dead when you hit her. And by the way, you didn't break her neck. The coroner would've spotted that. Huh-uh, you hit her, I guess, but you didn't kill her."

He nodded firmly. I reached for a cigarette, then dropped it to the floor unlit. And I was back there in the room with her, looking down on her body—her tense, stretched-out straight body—even her fingers stiff as dead wood. Dead, all right, that's what she was—and somehow I must have known it. Half of me, anyway, half of me must have known it. But the two-way pull had been working, and the other half had to keep at it, pushing and plunging and needling. So I hit her and picked her up and tossed her into the dog pound, *even though I knew she was dead.*

Christ.

His eyes softened a little. "She was a pretty lonely little lady, wasn't she, keed? From what I hear, she didn't get along with most people. So she was kind of nuts about you, and you didn't know how to stave her off and—well, maybe you'd better tell me what happened. Your guess would be better than mine. I figure she must have found out what was wrong with you. She must've seen that things weren't going to be like she'd thought. And I guess a little lady like that...I guess she couldn't take it. She didn't want to take it."

No one but you, Brownie. If I couldn't have you...

"You see, keed? Once I got that first murder out of the way, the real one, the others fell right into line. I could take 'em for what they were, a suicide and an accident."

"You don't know," I said. "You can't be sure. If I confessed to—"

"They'd put you in a nuthouse, Brownie. They wouldn't give you the gas chamber."

"Constance Wakefield was trying to blackmail me. I stalled her and got her to take that late train, and then I got on with her—"

"Save it, keed." He held up his hand. "I got a pretty good idea of what you did, and it don't make no difference, see? You didn't kill her. You didn't ride over into the next county and shove her off the train. It was just what it looked like—an accident."

"But I—I—"

"Okay," he shrugged. "Have it your own way. A couple years for assault and battery, six months for maiming a dead body, a couple of years more on this Wakefield deal—whatever they'd call that. About five years in the pen, say, if they believe you. That or the nuthouse. Is that what you want, keed?"

My throat was dry. I shook my head silently.

He sighed, and the sound was weary and a little sad. "It ain't much fun, is it, keed? You've been slidin' down the rope and havin' a hell of a time for yourself. And now you're at the bottom, and all you can do is hang there. You can't let go and you can't get anyone to give you a shove. It wouldn't make 'em nothing. They can't do your job for you. It—it ain't much fun, is it, keed?"

The Teletypes were clicking again. I turned and stared at them blankly, at the words marching across the yellow paper— across a vast and empty desert where a dead man walked through:

...TODAY'S WEATHER IN SOUTHERN AND LOWER CALIFORNIA. CLOUDY WITH THUNDER SHOWERS THIS MORNING, FOLLOWED BY...

"You know what I figured on doin', Brownie? Why I came up here? Well, I was goin' to give you the old horse laugh, keed. You were at the end of the line, I figured, and you'd be sittin' here waiting for someone to pick you off. Maybe you'd kidded yourself you was going to do a brodie, but I knew you wouldn't. You couldn't, any more'n you could have killed those other people. You'd make a pass at doin' it, but that'd be as far as it would go. You couldn't carry through with it. And like I been tellin' you, no one else is goin' to do it. There ain't going to be no pinch—no gas chamber. No easy way out. So I was going to lay it on the line for you, and watch you squirm. Make you beg like you've made me beg. Laugh at you like you've laughed at me. But—well, I'll tell you something, keed…"

…FOLLOWED BY CLEARING SKIES, STRONG TO MODERATE WINDS AND…

"…There's one thing about bein' a louse, keed. A no-good like maybe I am. When you're that way—"

"You're not that way," I said. "You're a long way from being a louse, Stuke. I don't know why I ever thought—"

"I'm telling you. When you're a louse yourself, keed, when you know you're a long way from being perfect yourself, the other lice don't look so bad to you. You're all in the same family, and you don't hurt 'em unless you have to. You don't make things no tougher on 'em than you have to. Look at me, Brownie." He gripped me by the shoulders. "I ain't laughin', am I? I didn't stay here to laugh. I'm here to help you."

He gave me a little shake, a brisk puffed-lipped nod of his head.

I said, "There's just one way you can help, Stuke. I—"

"Huh-uh," he said, firmly. "That's out, keed. I couldn't do it. I ain't goin' to. So forget it. You're goin' to snap out of it, Brownie. You're goin' to get your mind off of that—off of yourself, and start thinkin' about something else. That—it ain't everything. It—"

"Isn't it?" I said. "Isn't it rather easy for you to talk, Stuke?"

"It'd be easier not to, keed. A hell of a lot easier."

"But you don't know! You don't know what it's like to—"

"Keed"—he tapped me on the chest—"don't tell me what I

don't know. You'd be talking for the next forty years and we ain't got much time. You've got to get cleaned up, get yourself something to eat and a little sleep. You've got to be in here on the job in the morning, and you've got to work harder than you ever worked before. You're going to go on swinging your weight against the rats and the cheaters in this town, but this time you're going to swing it the right way. It ain't going to be a needle job. It's going to mean something.... Remember what I told you the other night? Well, I meant it. If the graft wasn't here to take, I wouldn't be taking it."

"But you don't know—I can't! God, how can I?"

"You ain't got no choice," he said.

His eyes were soft, sympathetic, friendly. They were firm and unwavering.

I looked away from him to the Teletype machines and the last lines of the weather forecast:

…THUNDER SHOWERS IN THE AFTERNOON. POSSIBLE CLEARING BY EVENING.

ABOUT THE AUTHOR

Jim Thompson (1906–1977), widely celebrated as America's "Dimestore Dostoevsky," was one of the most prolific crime-fiction writers of his generation. As a teenager, he sold his first story to *True Detective*, and he went on to write twenty-nine acclaimed novels. He also cowrote two original screenplays (for the Stanley Kubrick films *The Killing* and *Paths of Glory*). Several of his novels have been adapted into films, including the noir classics *The Killer Inside Me; After Dark, My Sweet;* and *The Grifters.*

...AND *THE KILLER INSIDE ME*

Mulholland Books also publishes Jim Thompson's *The Killer Inside Me*. Following is an excerpt from the novel's opening pages.

I

I'd finished my pie and was having a second cup of coffee when I saw him. The midnight freight had come in a few minutes before; and he was peering in one end of the restaurant window, the end nearest the depot, shading his eyes with his hand and blinking against the light. He saw me watching him, and his face faded back into the shadows. But I knew he was still there. I knew he was waiting. The bums always size me up for an easy mark.

I lit a cigar and slid off my stool. The waitress, a new girl from Dallas, watched as I buttoned my coat. "Why, you don't even carry a gun!" she said, as though she was giving me a piece of news.

"No," I smiled. "No gun, no blackjack, nothing like that. Why should I?"

"But you're a cop—a deputy sheriff, I mean. What if some crook should try to shoot you?"

"We don't have many crooks here in Central City, ma'am," I said. "Anyway, people are people, even when they're a little misguided. You don't hurt them, they won't hurt you. They'll listen to reason."

She shook her head, wide-eyed with awe, and I strolled up to

1

the front. The proprietor shoved back my money and laid a couple of cigars on top of it. He thanked me again for taking his son in hand.

"He's a different boy now, Lou," he said, kind of running his words together like foreigners do. "Stays in nights; gets along fine in school. And always he talks about you—what a good man is Deputy Lou Ford."

"I didn't do anything," I said. "Just talked to him. Showed him a little interest. Anyone else could have done as much."

"Only you," he said. "Because you are good, you make others so." He was all ready to sign off with that, but I wasn't. I leaned an elbow on the counter, crossed one foot behind the other and took a long slow drag on my cigar. I liked the guy—as much as I like most people, anyway—but he was too good to let go. Polite, intelligent: guys like that are my meat.

"Well, I tell you," I drawled. "I tell you the way I look at it, a man doesn't get any more out of life than what he puts into it."

"Umm," he said, fidgeting. "I guess you're right, Lou."

"I was thinking the other day, Max; and all of a sudden I had the doggonedest thought. It came to me out of a clear sky—the boy is father to the man. Just like that. The boy is father to the man."

The smile on his face was getting strained. I could hear his shoes creak as he squirmed. If there's anything worse than a bore, it's a corny bore. But how can you brush off a nice friendly fellow who'd give you his shirt if you asked for it?

"I reckon I should have been a college professor or something like that," I said. "Even when I'm asleep I'm working out problems. Take that heat wave we had a few weeks ago; a lot of people think it's the heat that makes it so hot. But it's not like

2

that, Max. It's not the heat, but the humidity. I'll bet you didn't know that, did you?"

He cleared his throat and muttered something about being wanted in the kitchen. I pretended like I didn't hear him.

"Another thing about the weather," I said. "Everyone talks about it, but no one does anything. But maybe it's better that way. Every cloud has its silver lining, at least that's the way I figure it. I mean, if we didn't have the rain we wouldn't have the rainbows, now would we?"

"Lou..."

"Well," I said, "I guess I'd better shove off. I've got quite a bit of getting around to do, and I don't want to rush. Haste makes waste, in my opinion. I like to look before I leap."

That was dragging 'em in by the feet, but I couldn't hold 'em back. Striking at people that way is almost as good as the other, the real way. The way I'd fought to forget — and had almost forgot — until I met her.

I was thinking about her as I stepped out into the cool West Texas night and saw the bum waiting for me.

2

Central City was founded in 1870, but it never became a city in size until about ten-twelve years ago. It was a shipping point for a lot of cattle and a little cotton; and Chester Conway, who was born here, made it headquarters for the Conway Construction Company. But it still wasn't much more than a wide place in a Texas road. Then, the oil boom came, and almost overnight the population jumped to 48,000.

Well, the town had been laid out in a little valley amongst a lot of hills. There just wasn't any room for the newcomers, so they spread out every whichway with their homes and businesses, and now they were scattered across a third of the county. It's not an unusual situation in the oil-boom country—you'll see a lot of cities like ours if you're ever out this way. They don't have any regular city police force, just a constable or two. The sheriff's office handles the policing for both city and county.

We do a pretty good job of it, to our own way of thinking at least. But now and then things get a little out of hand, and we put on a cleanup. It was during a cleanup three months ago that I ran into her.

"Name of Joyce Lakeland," old Bob Maples, the sheriff, told me. "Lives four-five miles out on Derrick Road, just past the old

Branch farm house. Got her a nice little cottage up there behind a stand of blackjack trees."

"I think I know the place," I said. "Hustlin' lady, Bob?"

"We-el," I reckon so but she's bein' mighty decent about it. She ain't running it into the ground, and she ain't takin' on no roustabouts or sheepherders. If some of these preachers around town wasn't rompin' on me, I wouldn't bother her a-tall."

I wondered if he was getting some of it, and decided that he wasn't. He wasn't maybe any mental genius, but Bob Maples was straight. "So how shall I handle this Joyce Lakeland?" I said. "Tell her to lay off a while, or to move on?"

"We-el," — he scratched his head, scowling — "I dunno, Lou. Just — well, just go out and size her up, and make your own decision. I know you'll be gentle, as gentle and pleasant as you can be. An' I know you can be firm if you have to. So go on out, an' see how she looks to you. I'll back you up in whatever you want to do."

It was about ten o'clock in the morning when I got there. I pulled the car up into the yard, curving it around so I could swing out easy. The county license plates didn't show, but it wasn't deliberate. It was just the way it had to be.

I eased up on the porch, knocked on the door and stood back, taking off my Stetson.

I was feeling a little uncomfortable. I hardly knew what I was going to say to her. Because maybe we're kind of old-fashioned, but our standards of conduct aren't the same, say, as they are in the east or middle-west. Out here you say yes ma'am and no ma'am to anything with skirts on; anything white, that is. Out here, if you catch a man with his pants down, you apologize... even if you have to arrest him afterwards. Out here you're a man, a man and a gentleman, or you aren't anything. And God help you if you're not.

The door opened an inch or two. Then, it opened all the way and she stood looking at me.

"Yes?" she said coldly.

She was wearing sleeping shorts and a wool pullover; her brown hair was as tousled as a lamb's tail, and her unpainted face was drawn with sleep. But none of that mattered. It wouldn't have mattered if she'd crawled out of a hog-wallow wearing a gunny sack. She had that much.

She yawned openly and said "Yes?" again, but I still couldn't speak. I guess I was staring open-mouthed like a country boy. This was three months ago, remember, and I hadn't had the sickness in almost fifteen years. Not since I was fourteen.

She wasn't much over five feet and a hundred pounds, and she looked a little scrawny around the neck and ankles. But that was all right. It was perfectly all right. The good Lord had known just where to put that flesh where it would *really* do some good.

"Oh, my goodness!" She laughed suddenly. "Come on in. I don't make a practice of it this early in the morning, but..." She held the screen open and gestured. I went in and she closed it and locked the door again.

"I'm sorry, ma'am," I said, "but—"

"It's all right. But I'll have to have some coffee first. You go on back."

I went down the little hall to the bedroom, listening uneasily as I heard her drawing water for the coffee. I'd acted like a chump. It was going to be hard to be firm with her after a start like this, and something told me I should be. I didn't know why; I still don't. But I knew it right from the beginning. Here was a little lady who got what she wanted, and to hell with the price tag.

Well, hell, though; it was just a feeling. She'd acted all right, and she had a nice quiet little place here. I decided I'd let her ride, for the time being anyhow. Why not? And then I happened to glance into the dresser mirror and I knew why not. I knew I couldn't. The top dresser drawer was open a little, and the mirror was tilted slightly. And hustling ladies are one thing, and hustling ladies with guns are something else.

I took it out of the drawer, a .32 automatic, just as she came in with the coffee tray. Her eyes flashed and she slammed the tray down on a table. "What," she snapped, "are you doing with that?"

I opened my coat and showed her my badge. "Sheriff's office, ma'am. What are *you* doing with it?"

She didn't say anything. She just took her purse off the dresser, opened it and pulled out a permit. It had been issued in Fort Worth, but it was all legal enough. Those things are usually honored from one town to another.

"Satisfied, copper?" she said.

"I reckon it's all right, miss," I said. "And my name's Ford, not copper." I gave her a big smile, but I didn't get any back. My hunch about her had been dead right. A minute before she'd been all set to lay, and it probably wouldn't have made any difference if I hadn't had a dime. Now she was set for something else, and whether I was a cop or Christ didn't make any difference either.

I wondered how she'd lived so long.

"Jesus!" she jeered. "The nicest looking guy I ever saw and

you turn out to be a lousy snooping copper. How much? I don't jazz cops."

I felt my face turning red. "Lady," I said, "that's not very polite. I just came out for a little talk."

"You dumb bastard," she yelled. "I asked you what you wanted."

"Since you put it that way," I said, "I'll tell you. I want you out of Central City by sundown. If I catch you here after that I'll run you in for prostitution."

I slammed on my hat and started for the door. She got in front of me, blocking the way.

"You lousy son-of-a-bitch. You—"

"Don't you call me that," I said. "Don't do it, ma'am."

"I did call you that! And I'll do it again! You're a son-of-a-bitch, bastard, pimp . . ."

I tried to push past her. I had to get out of there. I knew what was going to happen if I didn't get out, and I knew I couldn't let it happen. I might kill her. It might bring *the sickness* back. And even if I didn't and it didn't, I'd be washed up. She'd talk. She'd yell her head off. And people would start thinking, thinking and wondering about that time fifteen years ago.

She slapped me so hard that my ears rang, first on one side then the other. She swung and kept swinging. My hat flew off. I stooped to pick it up, and she slammed her knee under my chin.